FAE MATED

A CELESTIAL SOULS, INC. NOVEL

SHIFTED HEARTS
BOOK ONE

GODIVA GLENN

LUNAR MISCHIEF PRESS, L.L.C.

Fae Mated

Copyright © 2023 Godiva Glenn

Cover by Euphoric Designs

This is a work of fiction. Names, places, characters and incidents are either the product of the author's imagination or are used fictitiously, and any resemblance to any actual persons, living or dead, organizations, events or locales is entirely coincidental.

Follow Godiva Glenn at GodivaGlenn.com

❀ Created with Vellum

They might be meant for each other, but they're worlds apart ... literally

Who knew that saving a fae duke's life could earn you a one-way ticket to another planet? Brooke Donovan certainly didn't. But that's exactly what happens when she rescues one from a speeding car. Now, not only does she have to learn how to be a member of the royal court and acclimate to life on a magical new planet, but she must also deal with her overwhelming attraction to the duke—a man who fully intends to return to Earth, leaving Brooke galaxies away.

Duke Kerren Aodhan of Weylan Barrows never intended to return home. He'd been bored there for far too long and was ready to start fresh on Earth. But his near-death experience changed everything. Now obligated to help Brooke settle into her new life, Kerren has to return to his home on Sidera Luminis—at least temporarily. The return unearths more unseen obstacles, however. Mainly, can he keep his growing feelings for her from trapping him on his home world forever?

Circumstances seem determined to keep them apart, but fate (and an eccentric matchmaker named Euphrasie Hudson) has other ideas.

Fae Mated was previously published as Royally Screwed under MTWorlds Press. This is the author's new and preferred version.

CHAPTER 1

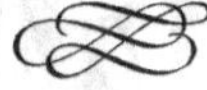

BROOKE

*B*rooke crossed her legs and sipped a sweet, iced tea while scanning the walkway outside the cafe. Each time a young man stopped and entered, she held her breath, wondering if her date had finally arrived. This was why she hated blind dates. The last thing she needed was to appear desperate, yet here she was, eagle eyes narrowing on every man not already attached to someone else.

She brushed at her peach dress, a fitted, sleeveless affair that clung to her curves in all the right ways. The soft color was one of her favorites, playing up her barely sun-kissed skin and new vibrant hair color. Just because she didn't want the date didn't mean she wasn't going to dress her best.

Looking up, she noticed a man in a sky-blue polo and khakis heading her way, attention focused on the red sweater she'd hung on the chair opposite her own. It was the flag, so to speak, in case he didn't recognize her from the photo.

He walked over, a smile on his face.

"Brooke?"

"That's me," she responded.

He sat, glancing around. She leaned forward to shake his

hand, and he took it reluctantly. Up close she noticed that his smile seemed stressed.

"Is something wrong?" she asked.

"No. Just wanted to make sure I had the right person," he said.

She sat back and slid a menu his way. "If there's another Brooke here with my face and sweater, I'd be running."

He nodded and frowned down at the menu. She studied him. The breeze blew over his stiffly pomaded blonde hair, not moving a single strand. His face was handsome but forgettable, as if there were such a thing as a perfect generic.

An expensive watch decorated his wrist and an onyx ring stood out like a mountain on his hand. His shoes looked like the sort billionaires wore on yachts.

Yet another reason she didn't like blind dates. Perhaps she didn't have a type, but she certainly had a 'not my type,' and this guy was it. *Be nice. Maybe he's really sweet.* Begrudgingly, she recalled the adage that opposites attract.

"So… Ethan, right?"

He blinked up at her. "Oh, sorry. Yeah. Ethan. Guess I'm a little out of sorts."

"Anna didn't mention what you do."

Holding his menu and leaning back in his seat he shrugged. "I like to think of myself as a renaissance man."

Oh, dear gods. She tried not to cringe outwardly. "Okay… go on?"

"I've tried my hand at a few things. I did accounting for years, great at it but I wanted something with more passion. I think my place is in business management."

"What sort of business?"

"Any. My dad's working on pulling some strings, listening around. Meanwhile, I've been moonlighting—I guess you could say—as a model."

Brooke's eyebrows threatened to lift high enough to

leave her face entirely. She cleared her throat and took a sip of her tea before responding, "I'm sorry—how do you know Anna?"

"She did my taxes last year and we kept in touch. I thought maybe we had something… you know, chemistry, but I guess then I wouldn't be here."

Brooke smiled and glanced down at her menu, even though she already knew what she wanted.

"Are you getting a salad?" he asked.

She pursed her lips and met his eyes. *Careful.* "I don't eat salad when I'm at a restaurant. I can rip apart lettuce and sprinkle dressing on it at home and save ten dollars."

"Yeah… I get it, I guess." Ethan tossed his menu on the table and leaned forward. "Look, your face is really pretty for a large woman, but you're not what I expected."

Brooke arched a brow. "Anna said you saw my picture. Though, I guess my hair was blonde then." She twirled a long, dark ruby tendril around her finger. "This is new. I think it's called 'Red Velvet.' Something delicious."

"It was just your face, and the angle…I guess there was cleavage, and don't get me wrong, I'm a boob guy, but that's a lot of—"

Her smile faded, and she released the lock of hair from her grasp. "You can go now."

"You don't have to take it personally. I support body positivity; I just can't see us doing things together. I'm a really active guy," he reasoned.

"Don't take it personally that I'm 'pretty for a large woman,' is that really what you think is body positive?" she asked calmly. She narrowed her blue eyes on him and allowed her usual resting bitch face to shine through. "You didn't even need to sit down and waste my time. You aren't doing me a favor by telling me to eat salad and revealing that you'd rather be banging Anna."

"Why are you being a bitch about it, I'm the one who was deceived."

"Are you still here? You need to walk away before you kill my appetite," she said coldly. "And you know I take food seriously."

He stood, face and composure annoyed. "Whatever."

She didn't bother watching him leave. Glancing over her shoulder, she flagged the waitress and ordered the chicken alfredo with a cup of the house tomato basil soup. She passed on the complimentary side salad.

Pulling out her phone, she composed a text in her head, something that would say *'what the fuck were you thinking?'* as politely as possible. Anna was her supervisor, after all. She couldn't burn that bridge, no matter how tenuous the support.

"It's a shame you had to waste even a minute of your time with that poor specimen of a man," a woman said from nearby. She'd stopped at Brooke's shoulder and peered down with twinkling gray eyes and a gentle smile. The sunlight glowed through her wild salt and pepper curls, giving her an almost ethereal appearance.

"I didn't realize I'd made a scene," Brooke admitted.

"You didn't. My hearing is just a little more sensitive than most." The woman extended a hand covered in gemstone rings and tinkling with large bangles around her wrist. "Euphrasie."

Brooke took the woman's hand and gave it a quick shake. "Brooke Donovan."

"May I sit?" Euphrasie asked. "The weather is gorgeous, and the patio is full. I'm just having some tea."

Brooke gestured to the empty seat. The stranger had an instant calming effect that she couldn't turn down. She'd barely spoken, but her voice was breezy and light, as if she'd never had a stressful moment in her life. Brooke could use that sort of energy. "Of course. I don't mind eating alone but I won't say no to the company."

The elder woman shook out the flowing green caftan she wore and sat. "Thank you." She fingered the menu and peered at Brooke. "Not to focus on something I'm sure you're eager to forget, but I'm in the dating business, and I absolutely hate to see a bad match."

"Which is why I wasn't looking for it."

"Oh?"

"It was a foolish set-up. My boss thought it would work, which is about par. Anna's a genius at her job, but her social skills are severely lacking."

"A shame. You handled it well enough. That's impressive." Euphrasie's head tilted. "Perhaps a professional matchmaker would do better?"

Brooke chuckled lightly. "Ah, thanks. But no. Between my job and the volunteer work I do for the historical society, I don't have time for dates."

"Except bad ones?" Euphrasie asked. "I'm kidding. There's nothing wrong with focusing on your career. And you said... historical society?"

"I handle tours, mostly. Occasionally pitch in at a fundraiser or two."

"Fascinating." Euphrasie smile grew, and her eyes sparkled as if she were plotting something. "But just between us, if you were ever to be in the market for a man, what interests you?"

The waitress returned, placing a hot aromatic tea before Euphrasie and arranging Brooke's pasta and soup on the table.

Brooke stirred the soup, a bit impressed by the woman's determination. "To be honest, I think I want too much. Luckily, if I'm meant to be alone, I'll cope."

"Nonsense. Granted, perhaps some people prefer solitude, but for those who wish it, there is someone for everyone." Euphrasie seemed to size Brooke up. "My clientele is different. Shifters, mostly. They tend to have a knack for having more than enough love."

"Love is nice. But the path to get there is the trick," Brooke replied. "I won't lie. I've met great men before—don't for a minute think that losers like Ethan make up the majority of my experience. I'm a curvy woman, but I usually attract the men who fawn over that."

Euphrasie nodded and took a delicate sip of her tea before motioning Brooke to continue. "But?"

"But," Brooke drew out the word, arranging her thoughts, "I may be expecting too much. I want to settle down, but I don't want to settle, if you know what I mean. I don't want to have a partner that makes me wonder 'what if,' I want someone who I know is the best for me, no doubts at all."

"That's how love should be. What are your expectations?"

"I want someone serious but fun. The kind of guy who will join me at fancy parties and not complain about wearing a tie but will do shots with me later when we're done schmoozing with co-workers. Classy when it's necessary but never arrogant. On top of that, he can't be afraid to step out of this city or this state, or this country for that matter, because I love exploring unfamiliar places and I've always wanted to share that."

"Go on," Euphrasie urged.

Brooke looked to the sky, imagining her dream catch. There was a guilty pleasure that came from sharing this with a stranger. Euphrasie didn't seem as judgmental as her friends, who regularly insisted that her perfect man wouldn't exist unless she dropped a few requirements.

Besides, there was something disarming about Euphrasie. Maybe the spiritual boho chic appearance combined with her age and the way she sounded relaxed and wise all at once. She was more apparition than human somehow. Brooke sensed she could confide anything with her.

"Sometimes men are sweet and doting, but in the wrong spirit. I'm not a delicate flower, and I hate being underestimated. The guy for me would care for me but not patronize me."

"None of these things sound like too much to me," Euphrasie said. She wafted her fingers over her tea and inhaled the steam for a moment before pinning Brooke with a mischievous grin. "But you're skipping the meat of the matter."

"Which is?"

"The sex, of course."

Brooke chuckled. "I knew I liked you. Yes, I want all the fabulous, passionate sex. So, you see, I want a sexy, smart, funny, talented lover. With his suitcases packed." She sighed. "A girl can dream."

Euphrasie sipped her tea and stared off thoughtfully. After a moment she nodded. "I guess you need someone out of this world."

CHAPTER 2

KERREN

"*D*id you even read the primer I gave you? You'll be in a portion of Earth designated as America. They're a relatively young civilization—"

"Vevina, relax. And of course, I didn't read your 'primer' because I can barely lift it. I've been to plenty of planets. I'll be fine," Kerren insisted, patting Vevina's shoulder and walking past her.

The loud clacking of determined heeled feet followed him down the corridor. Vevina stepped in his way with a huff. Her pale blue eyes narrowed, and she poked a single finger into his chest.

"Earth is not like other planets and this isn't like other trips. You want to live there, so you need to know the customs. I won't be there to help you adapt. This isn't a short trip," she said glaring. "I need to know that after I leave you with the representative, you won't somehow stumble into a war or get yourself jailed or similar."

He sighed loudly and rolled his shoulders. "Look. I under-stand your concern, but the wonderful thing is that I'll have my entire life to learn how things work. Besides, humans are humans, aren't they?"

He side-stepped her and strolled through his living room, into the kitchen where he grabbed an apple. "They have these, and the brochure is colorful. You should be excited for me. A new adventure."

Vevina snatched the apple from his hand, giving him a hard look. "Tell me you didn't choose your future home based on fruit."

He took the apple back from her and bit into it. Chewing the sweet fruit, he turned and leaned against the counter-top. He still needed to decide how to handle his home. Sidera Luminis didn't have too many fae that could afford it, but he didn't have any family to hand it over to.

"Kerren!"

He eyed his determined assistant, her mood so jolted that her hair had started to flicker colors to match—a feature of her genetics. It made it entertaining to toy with her. Truthfully, he'd done plenty of research regarding possible suitable homes on and off over the last few decades. He wasn't completely ignorant of the choice he'd made.

"I chose Earth because humans are unpredictable yet varied. The atmosphere is gentle on our systems, so I'll age slower but won't eventually die of some wild health disorder. It'll be easy for me to slide into a lifestyle and I get my pick of jobs, really. Being a duke has that perk, at least. All the string-pulling needed, in a world where a decent man could certainly be of use."

She settled down, hair returning to its usual soft peach tone. Crossing her arms, she looked around. "I can't believe you want to leave us."

"I'm not leaving you, personally. I'm leaving monotony. Sidera Luminis isn't enough for me. I'm bored. Earth is supposed to be full of life and surprises. It's not like I'm truly needed here. Which is exactly why I have this opportunity. Nobility with no ties to the crown of fae are free to leave."

"You're leaving family and friends to pursue a life of debauchery with humans," she accused.

"Is that so wrong?" He munched on the apple and waved his hand dismissively. "I'm kidding. Don't be like that. We both know that you've wanted a new job forever. Why not celebrate? You will no longer be bound to me until death. Your debt will dissolve, and you can do whatever you'd like."

She stared at him with her most unimpressed expression.

"I suggest dancer," he teased. "I love to watch you bounce around when you've had one too many glasses of wine."

She rolled her eyes and pulled out her electronic planner. "Your guide is situated in your desired city as we speak, native to the area and well-versed in the local customs. If we want to make a good impression, I suppose we should get going."

He nodded and tossed the apple core into the trash. After wiping the juice from his hand, he led the way towards the front door.

"I didn't think Earth had official representatives," he commented.

"They don't. However, I was able to track down a professional in the area, a Euphrasie Hudson."

"Never heard of her." He glanced over to Vevina, who stared down at her planner as she walked. "What's the nature of her profession?"

"Ah, she's a headhunter of sorts. Puts people in touch," Vevina replied. "She comes highly recommended."

"That's excellent work there. I'd give you a raise if it would go through before you were done working for me."

"There's such a thing as a bonus," she muttered under her breath.

Kerren grinned to himself. She would definitely get a

bonus, and he was eager to get his dream-come-true: A life outside the formal confines of Sidera Luminis.

THE PORTAL that connected Sidera Luminis to the rest of existence was an engraved wooden arch in the center of an open field, a device which upon cursory glance was nothing impressive given its capabilities. As Kerren and Vevina approached, vines climbed from the ground to encase the arch.

Reaching out, he fingered the strange flowers and leaves. "What are they?"

Vevina leaned forward, practically putting her nose into the bloom. She inhaled, then consulted her planner. "The red things are roses. The rest is an herb they call thyme."

"Fascinating," he said, stepping back to see the arch more clearly. "I always wonder how it decides the representation."

"You say that nearly every time," Vevina pointed out. "Except that one trip where the arch dripped with slime. That time, you were disgusted."

"It ruined my suit," he recalled.

She tucked her planner into her pocket and went to the fountain nearby. It ran with the water of reflections. While the arch itself managed travel, the water had to be ingested in order to ensure safe passage. It would also adjust their forms to be less flamboyant, since there were planets where the sight of an amber-skinned fae like Vevina could cause chaos.

She handed him a silver cup and he drank from it in one gulp. Handing it back, he shivered from the cold liquid coursing through his body. After she'd had her drink as well, they held hands and stepped through the arch.

Traveling through dimensions or across to different

planets took seconds, but always left Kerren feeling as if he'd lost hours of the day. To him, it was like taking a fifteen-minute nap and waking afraid that the entire day was gone.

Above, a bright sun shone down on them. He didn't look up, though it was nearly instinct to do so. Most planets didn't have dangerous lighting, but according to the brochure, looking directly at the burning sphere above him could rob him of sight.

He needed his sight.

Vevina handed him an envelope then. "Just put this in your pocket for now. It's your room key and instructions for appearing like an average guest."

"Room key? Are we on a building?" He tucked the envelope into his coat pocket.

She nodded. "The entryway from Sidera Luminis to Earth. We're on the roof of the Landsgate Faerriot. It's a luxury resort hotel and spa, according to the information here."

"That's perfect," he said with a grin. "See? Look at that sky. It's amazing here."

She made an unimpressed noise and gestured to a door in the distance. "You've been checked in automatically, so we really should get going if we're going to meet your guide for the next week."

"Only a week?"

"I'm sure that after that you can make arrangements. Maybe she could be talked into giving you more assistance after you've met," she said in a strange tone.

Kerren studied Vevina. Her stance seemed tense, her words sounded off. Normally her hair would shift colors to indicate her discomfort, whether she was lying or worried. But Vevina now looked human. Her peach hair was now a dull blonde, and her skin pale. Plain brown eyes blinked at him.

"Are you well?" he asked.

"I don't want to keep the human waiting. They have a tendency of being quite upset when left expecting. Duels have been fought," she replied.

"Fine, fine." He started towards the door. "What's her name, then?"

"Ms. Brooke Donovan."

KERREN DID his best to analyze everything about their journey to the designated meeting place. He studied street signs, observed the clothing of those around him, and tried to picture what an average day would be like once he was settled in.

Will I sit outside drinking tea? Will I pretend that coffee is palatable in order to fit in better? What sort of friends will I make?

The possibilities were all in the air, waiting for him to leap into action.

They exited their borrowed transportation after Vevina explained their currency system. The car ride had been pleasant, but the vehicle itself was nowhere near as aesthetically pleasing as the ones in the brochure.

"I need to find something suitable for my tastes." He watched the car leave. "Something sleek. And dark green. I'm not fond of these boring colors."

Vevina had her planner open in a heartbeat, skimming the electronic database. "It appears that luxury vehicles are rarely produced in shades of green. A few sporty ones come in this sickly neon, but I imagine what... something more like a deep emerald?"

"Emerald would be perfect. Why no green? They have blue and red. I believe I saw a purple one on the way."

She shrugged. "I can continue looking later—you need to learn to drive first."

He unbuttoned his suit jacket and took a deep breath. The warm weather fit the scene before him. Pink flowers bloomed on the trees and leaves of bright green swayed. He watched a family wander by and his heart tugged a bit. *Will I get that too?*

A splash of color in the crowd of people stood out. Bright scarlet hair poured down the back of a curvy figure, and as she turned, Kerren's pulse raced. Bold roses and leaves decorated her front and back in an hourglass pattern, further emphasizing her ample chest as it had her round ass.

She walked toward them, hips swaying, long legs accentuated by the fitted floral dress and flesh-toned high heels. Her hair danced in the breeze and matched her red painted lips.

As she drew closer, he saw the bright aquamarine hue of her eyes. For a human, she looked positively radiant. Though there were beautiful women scattered around, this one had a tangible presence.

The curve of her lips made him swallow. Her smile was wicked and sweet at the same time, and terribly distracting. He'd never before seen a mouth and instantly wondered how divine it would be to kiss. How naughty it would look around his cock.

"Vevina? Mr. Aodhán?" she asked upon reaching them, looking at each of them expectantly, voice slapping Kerren from his fantasy.

Vevina shook the woman's hand enthusiastically. "Ms. Donovan, it's a pleasure to meet you."

Trying not to stare, Kerren offered his hand as neutrally as possible. Her voice was gently husky, a sultry music to his ears. "Ms. Donovan, my pleasure... but please, it's just Kerren. No mister required."

"In that case, call me Brooke."

He looked down at her fragile hand in his. Bending forward slightly, he lifted her hand by the fingertips and kissed the back gently. It wasn't a formality that felt necessary, except that he wanted to kiss her.

Vevina nudged his side and he released Brooke's hand. Brooke had a stunned expression but didn't look offended.

"Oh," she said softly. "I was told you would be… different."

"Different?" he asked.

Her cheeks blazed bright pink and she licked her lips. "I mean, not in an offensive way. Just… well, I've been doing this for a while and I've never met fae royalty. Actually, I'm not sure I've met many fae at all, if any."

"We like our privacy. We tend to get more attention than, say, your average run-of-the-mill bear shifter," Vevina explained.

"Besides, I'm nobility, not royalty," Kerren interrupted.

"I don't remember the difference," Brooke admitted.

"Royalty is in the blood. Nobility is in the title," he summarized. "It may be the same way on Earth, but I don't recall. One of the things I like about America though, fewer complicated titles."

Brooke smiled at his words and turning her head she motioned to the trees around them. "Blood and titles aside, I was told that fae often miss the more natural aspect of home, so I aimed to begin our tour here.

"It's magnificent," Kerren remarked, though his eyes never left Brooke.

She swiveled on her heel and tilted her head. "This way then. The park leads into the botanical gardens, and you happen to be with an unofficial tour guide of the grounds. The current exhibit is butterflies, so it should be fun."

"I thought the tour would be of the city," Vevina pointed out.

"Of course," Brooke said. "But this is the heart of the city.

I don't mean to overstep my bounds, I simply felt it would be a place of comfort. Unless you drive out of the city, you won't see nature like this."

Kerren smiled. "I believe I know what you mean. I'll miss my gardens from home, so I imagine I'll visit this area often." He took a step forward. "Please lead the way. I'd love to see more of Earth's beauties."

CHAPTER 3

BROOKE

The setting sun alerted Brooke to just how long they'd toured the gardens. Kerren was fascinating company. He was curious about everything they saw, and his interest was beyond killing time and making conversation.

He compared each flower, tree, and shrub to something from his home, the fae planet of Sidera Luminis. She doubted the average person knew as much about a sunflower as he seemed to know about the herbology of his home.

And as if his mind wasn't enough, he looked like sex on a stick drenched in hot fudge. She swore that the moment he'd kissed her hand, her ovaries exploded.

Tall, strong guys always did it for her. She loved a guy who could pick her up and wouldn't require her to wear flats. At five-foot-eight she was already tall, but pair that with four-inch heels and suddenly she was towering over most of her past boyfriends.

Kerren caught her staring, his hazel eyes sparkling. Throughout the day he'd looked at her with an expression that felt teasing, but she knew she wasn't the butt of a joke. Rather, he seemed to have a joking side that wanted to come out. Hidden behind the layers of quiet formality and gentle-manly manners.

"We seem to have exhausted the sun," he commented.

"That happens. Something about time flying when you're having fun," she replied.

He nodded, and it made his mahogany brown hair bounce in the breeze. For some reason when she envisioned faeries she saw them as paler, or wildly colored. Kerren had olive skin and nothing about his appearance even hinted at him being anything but human. Same with Vevina.

Not that Brooke had ever met a human that made her knees weak with just his appearance and the low accented sound of his voice. Not even close.

She led them to the exit, one hand on her rumbling stom-ach. Time had slipped by, but once she acknowledged it, her body had awoken. It was ravenous.

"Tomorrow we can visit downtown. I know all the land-marks," she said.

"I look forward to it," Kerren replied.

Vevina followed them both, appearing more interested in her handheld planner than anything else. She wasn't moving to Earth, after all.

"Did you need a ride back to wherever you're staying?" Brooke asked.

"I thought we'd walk," Kerren stated. "The drive was short. The hotel can't be too far."

"Cars move much faster than you think," Vevina reasoned. "I'd rather not spend the next hour lost on the streets."

Brooke smiled. "I would be happy to drop you off. Then I'd know where to meet up with you in the morning."

"That seems fair," Kerren agreed. "It's the Landsgate Faerriot."

"Oh, yeah, that's more than a brisk walk." Brooke made

her way down the steps from the garden's main entrance and pointed across the street. "I'm parked right over this way."

They walked while Vevina and Kerren chatted about evening plans. Brooke glanced down into her purse, digging for her keys once they reached the crosswalk. The sound of honking cars made her head jerk up. Kerren had stepped off the pavement, directly into traffic.

She grabbed Kerren's arm and tugged him towards her with every ounce of strength. He tumbled back from the road and they both landed on the ground. The cars sped by, never hesitating.

"Why were you in the road?" she gasped. She sat on the sidewalk, brushing hair from her face. Her blood rushed, making her alert yet tingly. "You could have been killed!"

Kerren stared at the cars zooming by, not saying a word.

Vevina knelt by him. "Kerren," she hissed. She shook his shoulders. "Have you lost your mind?"

"I..." He rubbed his eyes and shook his head. "Damn. I assumed they'd stop."

"No, they'd sooner run you over," Brooke explained. "You have to wait for the light."

He looked at her as if coming from a trance. "Are you hurt? Tell me my foolishness didn't get you injured?"

"I'm fine."

He stood shakily then offered her a hand up. As she stood he pulled her close, wrapping his strong arms around her and holding her tightly. The sudden embrace made her rushing blood slow and calm, as if nothing was wrong. Everything felt perfectly right, in fact. Beneath his suit hid lean muscle, the thought of which made her shiver. She took a deep breath, inhaling his scent, a strange blend of herbs and smoke.

"I'm so sorry, Brooke."

"It's fine... I mean, don't run into traffic again, but I guess

I should've said something about the proper—"

"Is your dress alright?" He held her at arm's length and looked her over.

His scrutiny made her blush, but she wasn't sure why. "It's fine."

He scowled, but his silence suggested it was aimed at himself.

"The lights…" Vevina said softly.

Brooke glanced towards the pedestrian signal. "Ah. See how it's a man walking?"

Kerren looked up but said nothing. Brooke took his hand and led him forward. Vevina rushed across ahead of them.

Safely on the other side, she released Kerren's hand. He didn't seem fully recovered. It had to be hard to be in a new place, and harder to grasp how a tiny mistake could end up with dire consequences.

"Kerren?" she asked.

He turned to her, seeming to snap out of his daze. "Join us for dinner? I owe you much more."

He took her hand again and waited patiently. It took her a moment to realize they were waiting on her. She led them to her car, Kerren squeezing her hand gently.

Sitting behind the wheel, her heart sped anew. The reality of what had almost happened caught up with her. Day one of introducing a fae duke to her city, and he'd almost become roadkill.

She half expected her phone to ring and find a pissed off Euphrasie on the other end. What else could go wrong?

BROOKE WALKED into the lobby of the Landsgate Faerriot with curiosity blazing. She'd never been inside before, and even if she knew to expect luxury, the hotel was more than she could have imagined.

Her pumps clicked against the glossy tile floor, a masterpiece of creamy white with black inlaid swirls. Crystal chandeliers lined the length of the room, casting a soft glow down on the ivory marble columns. A fountain topped with bright coral blooms stood center, the only splash of true color.

She could only guess what the rooms looked like.

"This is gorgeous," she breathed.

Kerren stood next to her, following her gaze. "You've never seen it?"

"No reason to visit, really. Not like I'd have reason to stay in a hotel in the city I call home."

"But you know the rest of the city."

"I know the historical areas. The history around this building is oddly vague." She took a few steps forward then turned back to him. "I just realized. Faerriot. Fae-rriot. It's a fae hotel?"

He nodded. "Which is probably why the official past is vague, as you say."

She shook her head, amused that she'd never suspected it before. Usually, she was quick to notice connections. For now, she observed that Kerren appeared unimpressed with the room they stood in, suggesting that Sidera Luminis had plenty of splendor. As a duke, most of the modern human world would be dull, she imagined.

Wealth was something she didn't judge but had often felt slighted by. Most of the guys with money tended to act like it. Entitled, snooty, arrogant. Men like Ethan.

With Kerren, she kept forgetting he was rich. He was charming but not condescending. His suit appeared to be custom and have cost a small fortune, yet throughout the day he'd knelt in the grass and sat on dirty benches. He put her at ease instead of making her put up her guard.

She hadn't known what to expect when she agreed to Euphrasie's request. Working as a personal liaison for a duke had sounded as exciting as it was daunting.

"Okay. They're ready. It took some sweet-talking, but I got you two the best seats in the restaurant," Vevina announced, appearing at Kerren's side.

"Us two?" Kerren asked in a confused tone.

Brooke frowned slightly. "You're not joining us?"

Vevina waved a hand. "Oh no. You seem to have everything under control. Actually, I'm heading back to Sidera Luminis."

"Already?" Kerren crossed his arms. "Abandoning me?"

"You know I'm not a fan of the human world. I caught myself in the mirror and nearly died. I can't live like this." She offered Brooke an apologetic smile. "It was very nice meeting you. Perhaps we'll meet again sometime."

Brooke wanted to ask what the mirror had to do with anything, but Vevina was clearly in a rush to leave. She took the small woman's hand and shook it. "If you're ever around, definitely."

Kerren gave Vevina a hug, a distinct look of sadness softening his serious face. They whispered to each other while Brooke tried not to eavesdrop. Not that it mattered—they spoke in a language like nothing she'd ever heard.

"I just have a few things to do before I go, but if you need me, use the phone I left in your suite," Vevina said, pulling away and appearing to study Kerren's expression. "Phone. The black rectangle... the... Brooke can explain it to you. It's how humans communicate when they aren't together."

Kerren rolled his eyes. "I'm not a child."

Vevina pursed her lips.

"I'd be happy to look at it and help you figure it out," Brooke offered.

Vevina gave them each a smile. Brooke turned to peek at

the restaurant, and when she turned back, Vevina was gone. Kerren stepped up beside her.

"Shall we?"

She nodded. He crooked his arm and she slipped her hand into it, surprised at the action but eager to hold him. He was strange and new, exactly what she needed to keep her mind off her current man-less situation.

Part of her regretted not asking Euphrasie to set her up. In the week since her horrid blind date, she'd felt unusually antsy for companionship. Being up close to a handsome fae like Kerren was practically torture.

THE RESTAURANT within the hotel served mostly Italian dishes, much to Brooke's surprise and utter delight.

The chicken alfredo was thick and decadent, and so delicious that she was tempted to lick her plate clean. She swirled the last of her steamed broccoli through the creamy sauce and somewhat mourned that she'd eaten so fast. Her eyes closed as she savored the last bite, and when she opened them again realized Kerren was staring—and she'd been moaning.

"It was so good," she said sheepishly.

"I'm glad you enjoyed it. Are we thinking dessert?" Kerren asked eyeing her empty plate. "I think we need chocolate or ice cream or something…"

Brooke grinned, embarrassment slipping away. "Do you have a sweet tooth?"

"I'm eager to try new things." He sipped his wine and traced his fingers up and down the long stem of the glass, appearing to want to say more. "I've traveled plenty, but I've never felt as out of my element as today."

"I can only imagine how different it is."

He offered a crooked smile. "Sidera Luminis is... I suppose it would be like your French renaissance mixed with Gaelic lore. Incidentally, we and a few other fae civilizations directly influenced that." Swirling the wine in his glass gently, he continued, "I think the biggest difference is the atmosphere. Sidera Luminis feels lighter, like the magic lifts you somewhat."

"And you're a duke... so why would you leave?" she asked. Immediately after asking, she regretted it. It wasn't her business.

His only response was a shrug, and they sat in silence until the waiter came to give the dessert options. They opted to split a New York cheesecake, since Kerren had never tried such a thing.

After the waiter left, Brooke reached across the table and brushed her fingertips to Kerren's. "I'm sorry," she said. "I sometimes speak before I think. Whatever you're doing here, it's not my place to inquire."

He laced their fingers together, staring at her hand while his mind seemed to work. She could practically see the cogs turning.

"Sidera Luminis is beautiful, but it is not perfect. The life of a duke isn't magical, really. The restrictions tend to outweigh the perks."

"Like what? I can't imagine what restrictions could be so terrible," she admitted. She half-prepared for his argument, expecting him to equate riches and luxury with prison, the way celebrities wanted to be 'normal people.'

"For example, if I were to see a lovely woman like you, I couldn't spend time with her unless she was of a certain house and breeding. Then, all noble matches have to be blessed by the King and Queen."

That was unexpected. "What?"

"A couple could fall in love, only to have that love decided as unworthy. I suppose many think it's an acceptable restraint, but it left my parents in a loveless union."

"I'm sorry." Brooke hated the idea of seeking approval like that. Her parents had hated every guy she'd dated through high school and college, but it's not like they were in charge of her decisions in the end.

"It made me less than eager to find a woman for myself." He glanced up, the golden undertones of his eyes glowing in the candlelight. "Not that I've ever encountered a woman like you before."

"Oh?"

"From the moment I first saw you, your hair was like a beacon. So vibrant and alluring."

"It's not natural."

"So? It's your personality, isn't it?" He pulled her fingertips and placed his palm against hers, fully holding her hand. "It's more than that, however. You have a regal bearing. Confidence that has a glow."

Her cheeks grew warm, and she knew they were as red as her hair. "Ah. Well, thank you."

"And you're gorgeous."

The waiter deposited the chocolate drizzled cheesecake between them and left.

Brooke didn't know how to respond. Wit escaped her. Flirting usually came second-nature to her, but Kerren disarmed her. He'd just more or less stated that he'd left his world to find freedom and love, and then hit on her.

"I bet you say that to all the ladies that save your life," she teased finally.

He arched a brow but released her hand and picked up his fork. "So, this is cheesecake."

CHAPTER 4

KERREN

*K*erren walked beside Brooke, escorting her out of the restaurant and into the lobby. His hand twitched at his side, wanting to rest on the small of her back and bring her closer.

His brush with mortality had left him shaken and he rallied for recovery. On Sidera Luminis, he was mostly immortal. On Earth, he was mostly human.

The timing couldn't have been worse. He had a plan to keep Brooke around, but everything had fallen apart now. His usual organic charm had gone into hiding. He was floundering for a way to tell her how intoxicatingly enchanting she was.

His human guise wasn't helping, really. Like Vevina, a glimpse in the mirror had left him shaken. He didn't recognize himself and didn't like what he saw. His human face was handsome, but it wasn't really him. It felt like a lie.

Brooke came to a stop and looked at the doorway. She'd accepted his compliment, she'd shared a dessert, but he still wasn't sure where he stood. He wanted to see her again, no, needed to. He recalled how she felt in his arms, soft and warm.

"We'll continue tomorrow?" he asked.

She nodded. "I'm looking forward to it." Her eyes took in the room again. "I'll meet you here?"

There was a hesitation in her voice, and he realized that his worries were remnants of the earlier incident. She had enjoyed his company, and he was anxious for no reason. He was Kerren Aodhán, Duke of Weylan Barrows, not insecure riff-raff.

He placed a hand on her chin and steadied her wandering gaze, seeking to be the sole focus of her radiant blue eyes. It worked, and she studied him with what suggested a mixture of curiosity and anticipation.

Stepping close, he removed the space between them and kissed her. She was sweet and eager, and the softest sigh escaped her lips as he gripped her waist to keep her near. Everything about her was perfect. The way she clung to his jacket, the way she pressed her large breasts against him, the floral perfume of her.

After a moment she pulled back, eyes glued to his mouth. "You've got lipstick on you. Sorry."

He frowned. "Don't apologize. It should be me apologizing for messing you up." His thumb swept at a streak of red trailing towards her chin. "Though I'm only partially sorry."

"If I even suspected… I wouldn't have worn lipstick at all."

"Suspected what? That you'd be manhandled?"

She smiled mischievously. "I wouldn't call this manhandled, but I wouldn't say no to such a thing."

"You shouldn't tempt me. If you give me an invitation, I don't know where we'll end up. It was hard enough keeping my hands to myself this long."

Her blue eyes widened with faux innocence. "Aww… but I like it when it's hard."

Kerren exhaled and closed his eyes, drawing upon every ounce of strength to refrain from ripping her clothes off and taking her on the polished tile floor, even if it would kill his knees.

Massaging the nape of her neck, he tangled his hand in her soft hair. He tugged down, and she lifted her chin.

"I could kiss it and make it better," she whispered. "If it's that… hard."

That was the final straw. He growled and dragged her to the elevator. "I think we should explore this matter someplace more private."

She kept quiet until he'd punched in the floor number and they started to ascend, then she gave him a look that tore his patience. He pinned her to the mirrored wall and pushed her thick, deep ruby hair aside, so he could kiss her beautiful neck.

The noises she made stirred his blood into a fine frenzy until he was rock hard and having trouble thinking. It usually took more than a nice body and a kiss to get him this aroused. Brooke had cast a spell on him, there was no doubt.

Already he was lost in imagining the moment he sank his length into her. The elevator chimed, and they tumbled into the hall. He cursed as he realized he didn't recall his room number. Digging around his pocket, he glanced left and right, but since he hadn't yet been to his room, nothing was familiar.

The key, as Vevina had called it, was a bit of rigid plastic in the shape of a flat rectangle. There was no designation on it, just the floral logo of the hotel. He took a second look at the envelope it was in and noticed no room number, just the words 'Gilded Hawthorne Suite.'

"That sounds fancy," Brooke commented, eyeing the envelope.

"But where is it," he grumbled.

She took the envelope from him and dug around while he continued to examine his key.

"There's a map," she said triumphantly. "We're... on the wrong floor."

"Of course."

They piled back into the elevator and headed up. He was silently grateful for the brief intermission since he wanted a somewhat clear head before touching Brooke again. He wanted to recall every lavish detail.

The door opened, and Brooke led the way, hips swaying dangerously. He bit the inside of his lip to maintain his focus as he followed.

"Here." She stopped and stepped aside.

He held the key out, uncertain. "And this goes where?"

She took his wrist and waved the key across a silver metal pad. A click sounded, and he was able to turn the knob. Swinging the door inward, he placed a hand on her back and guided her in.

BASED ON THE LOW 'WOW' that Brooke exhaled upon stepping into the room, Kerren assumed the suite was to her liking. His own attention was solely on locating a bed.

Brooke turned and grabbed Kerren's tie, using it to yank him into a kiss. They moved through the room together until the back of her knees hit the arm of an ivory sofa. His hand moved over the bottom of her dress, but it was too tight to budge, ruining his plan to hike it up.

"Zipper," she said, coming up for air.

"Right. Zipper…"

She turned her back to him and bent slightly forward onto the sofa. The motion put her round ass directly on his hardened cock, which strained enough in his pants to cause more than a slight amount of discomfort. Gripping her waist, he pressed his erection against her and groaned.

"Zipper," she repeated.

He shook his head, freeing himself from the daze. The zipper pull was well hidden, but once he found it and tugged down, it was worth the hassle. The fabric parted, revealing her pale skin contrasted against the black lace of her undergarments.

She wriggled free of the dress, letting it fall to the floor. While kissing her shoulder he trailed his fingertips along her smooth flesh.

"Stunning," he whispered.

One hand on his belt and leading him, she stepped around the sofa and sat. She tugged the buckle loose, but he covered her hands with his.

"I want to taste you," he said, dropping to his knees before her.

"But that's what I want."

He didn't respond, instead kissing the tops of her breasts and cupping the overflowing mounds with his hands. The pink hue of her nipples sneaked through the sheer floral pattern of her bra, teasing him.

She was a work of art, and he didn't plan on rushing. He sucked one of the hard tips into his mouth, nibbling through the fabric until her head fell back and she gasped.

Moving down, he kissed her stomach and toyed with the top band of her underwear. He yanked her towards the front of the sofa and spread her legs wider, until he could see the triangle of black lace.

He kissed her through the barrier, licking the patterned

cloth while she squirmed above him. His index finger hooked the wet fabric and pulled it aside, revealing her folds. Moisture glistened on them and he dove in, lapping up her sweet arousal.

She moaned from above him, fingers digging into his hair.

"You're finer than chocolate and wine," he teased. "I could eat this sweet pussy all night."

There was no reply, only a tremble that ran along her body, shaking her soft thighs. He pressed the tip of his tongue to her slit, opening her. Her slick juices and velvety folds tested his restraint. As much as he wanted to sink his cock into her, he wondered if perhaps he was taking advantage of her.

She was somewhat of his employee at this moment. It didn't escape him that everything about this was wrong, but he could only control himself so much.

He circled his tongue around her clit, drawing more moaning and shaking. Her body was obscenely responsive, and it only fueled his hunger for her. His mind was made. Tonight, he would pleasure her until she could no longer speak, and they could discuss the rest in the morning.

"Don't stop," Brooke whimpered.

"I wouldn't dream of it," he promised.

He plunged two fingers into her wet entrance and sucked the swollen bud of her clit into his mouth. The room filled with the sweet sounds of her ecstasy. There was no restraint in her voice as every lick and suck was met with pleasured cries and demands for more. He became obsessed with her insatiable needs.

The tight walls of her pussy spasmed around his fingers and pride filled his chest. He continued to torment her throughout her orgasm, until she tried to escape. He held her down and latched onto her, exploring her with his mouth until she shook again and again, until her moans became hoarse.

He rose to kiss her, though his fingers still pumped in and out of her quivering heat. She didn't shy away from the moisture on his lips, sharing her flavor as their tongues battled.

"I want to taste you," she begged.

"I want everything to be about you," he replied. "I want you to come until you've forgotten your name and only remember mine."

She laughed softly. "Can't we compromise?"

Kerren slipped his fingers from her depths and shrugged. "Recline against the arm and touch yourself."

She shifted over as instructed and he took a deep breath, momentarily lost at the sight of his goddess. Delightfully naughty, she squeezed a breast in one hand while the other massaged her pussy.

"Damn. Very good," he breathed.

"It feels good," she whispered.

He yanked his belt free and undid his pants, shoving them down. He wore nothing underneath—he didn't understand the unnecessary layers of human clothing—and his erection sprang free, eliciting an approving coo from Brooke.

Moving to the end of the couch where she reclined, he pumped his length in his fist. She turned her head and licked her lips. He offered himself eagerly, closing his eyes the moment her soft tongue teased the head of his cock.

Her mouth closed around him, sucking hungrily. Tangling her hair around his fingertips, he stifled a moan, determined to last. Except it had been too long since he'd been touched this way, and his blood had been racing most of the day.

Getting Brooke off had nearly made him spill in his pants. She was too sexy to resist, and he was powerless to her charms. The way she moaned around his thick length uncurled the pleasure that had been building. He wanted to give her what she wanted.

One of her hands reached out and gripped him at the base, making him grit his teeth. He watched her fingers pumping in and out of her wet pussy, and it was enough to tip the scales of his self-control. A searing jolt tore down his spine and he groaned as he spilled thick ribbon after ribbon of cum over her smiling lips.

The room spun, and her tongue swirling around the head of his cock, collecting every last drop, made his knees weak. Never before had a woman given him pleasure this intense, bordering on enough to leave him comatose. And that had just been her mouth.

"Mmmm," she moaned. "I think we're almost even."

He shook his head, partially in disagreement and partially to clear the fog and regain his footing.

"I won't stop until we are nowhere near even," he promised.

CHAPTER 5

BROOKE

*B*rooke sat up with a jolt.

"Damn," she breathed, running her hands through her hair. Without even having to look at the clock, she knew she'd overslept. She hopped from the bed and paused. This wasn't her room.

The previous nights' events came tumbling back to her. Kerren had insisted she spend the night, since he'd given her enough orgasms to make her incoherent. He'd even followed her into the shower and fingerbanged her until she was a shaking mess on the tile floor.

Not that she was complaining, not in the slightest.

Still, she had to get into her office today and put in a few hours of work before returning and taking Kerren out on the town. If they made it out of the room, that was.

It was tempting to just do to him what he'd done to her. She knew a few tricks that would keep him from walking for hours. She licked her lips, recalling the salty taste of him on her tongue.

"Good morning," a voice called.

The light flipped on and Brooke screamed, pulling the

blanket over her naked body. Seated atop the dresser facing the bed was a strange small woman in a pink dress, staring at her.

Kerren ran in, having slept on the couch after tucking Brooke into his bed. He looked around the room, eyes wild. "What's going on?"

"Royal summons," the stranger announced cheerfully.

Kerren stood between Brooke and the woman. "You can't summon me, Lorelei. The court has no say over my life as long as I'm in the human realm."

The stranger, Lorelei, it seemed, sighed and leaned to the side to peer around Kerren at Brooke.

"Ms. Brooke Donovan, you are officially summoned to the court of King Artur and Queen Catriona. You are expected within the hour, and since it is upon short notice and you are human, we are waiving the formal codes..." Lorelei looked Brooke over with a mischievous smirk. "You may wear whatever attire you have available."

Brooke sputtered and pulled the blanket tighter around her body. Stepping next to Kerren, she noted the tense line of his jaw. "I don't understand. Did we do something wrong?"

A million possibilities flew through her mind. *Was it illegal to have spent the night with a fae duke? Am I considered a human commoner?* Surely this was just a misunderstanding.

"We didn't have intercourse," she blurted.

Lorelei's brows lifted so high they disappeared beneath her blonde bangs. "That's neither here nor there, Ms. Donovan."

"But we, I mean—"

Kerren placed an arm around her and tilted her head towards him with his gentle hand, silencing her. "It wasn't that, Brooke. Even if we had... there are no rules against that. Not here, at least." He glanced at Lorelei. "What is this concerning? Since when does the court call upon humans?"

"The matter in question has to be resolved before it becomes a concern, Your Grace. Regardless, you are not within any rights to keep us from following fae law," she replied tartly. "Ms. Donovan will appear at court or we will bring her in."

"Bring me in?" Brooke asked defensively.

"Please understand, this is a high honor. Most humans will never see the glory of Sidera Luminis's Pure court, and you are being invited to meet the King and Queen. Is there a reason you'd want to turn that down?" Lorelei asked, tone noticeably more generous. "I assure you this isn't something we take lightly. You will be treated with the utmost respect as a guest of the court."

Brooke looked up at Kerren, but he was glaring solidly at Lorelei. The chance to see his world sounded too good to be true, even if the circumstances were confusing.

"Is it safe?" she asked him.

"They can't harm you. Even if you did something wrong —which you certainly haven't—there are rules. It goes without saying, I will accompany you."

Brooke rubbed her temple, feeling overwhelmed. "No. Wait. I can't do this. I have work. I'm already late, in fact. There's no way they're going to accept the excuse that... shit. Would I even be allowed to tell them I was summoned to a fae planet?"

She shook her head, answering herself. "No. Definitely not, even if they believed me they'd want to know what I did to be in trouble on another planet—"

"You aren't in trouble," Lorelei corrected. "There are simply questions."

"Just ask me now, then."

"That's not how it works. I'm just a lowly messenger," Lorelei explained.

"Bullshit," Kerren muttered. "You're Catriona's personal page."

Brooke's jaw dropped. Whatever they wanted her for, it seemed to be a big deal.

Lorelei hmphed and slid from the dresser where she'd perched. "Your employer will be handled, and you will incur no repercussions from missing a day of work."

"Right," Brooke said sarcastically. She could just imagine Lorelei trying to talk to her piece of work boss.

Lorelei narrowed her eyes. "Anna Petersburg, senior accountant for Stonewolf Industrial Supply. Your boss has already been notified."

"But…"

Kerren worked a hand through his hair. "I'm sorry, Brooke. If she says it's handled, it has been. We have some pull here."

"Why are you sorry?" she asked.

"Because we need to go. You can't ignore a summons. Even I can't think of a loophole to get you out of it. But I'll be with you."

Frustration bubbled beneath everything else. "Look. Yes, I want to see another world, but I don't appreciate strangers interfering in my life," she bristled, looking at Lorelei. "And I definitely didn't like being ordered around by a royal family I have never even heard of before today!"

"I'm just the messenger," Lorelei replied. "I'll leave and let you make yourself presentable. If Sir shall accompany miss Donovan, then there's no reason for me to hang around."

"See yourself out," Kerren advised her coldly.

Lorelei walked out of the bedroom and Kerren shut the door behind her.

"I don't know what this is about, Brooke, but I promise there's a reasonable explanation. We'll get to the bottom of it, and we'll return here, and we'll move on from it."

"Can she really drag me to Sidera Luminis? She's so tiny," Brooke muttered sitting on the edge of the bed.

He sat next to her. "I don't know how they'd handle it, to be completely honest. But if they say they can force you to go, it's possible they would enlist human authorities."

"The police?"

"They work together when necessary, I'd imagine."

She ran a hand through her tangled red locks. "I guess I better shower again."

"Really…" he whispered, waggling his brows.

"Nope. Hands off," she said, clucking her tongue as she rose. "You are not going to make me late." She went into the bathroom and called out, "If I'm going to meet a King and a Queen today, even if not by choice, I'm going to look good and I'm going to be on time."

"Time doesn't matter," he said. "Sidera Luminis doesn't run on the same clock. I'm sure she just said 'within the hour' to sound formal. When we step through the portal, chances are it'll be night."

She peeked through the doorway. "Oh."

"Besides, if I'm going to accompany you, we'll need to stop by my home. I must change into something more befitting the occasion. The rules may bend for you, but I have to dress the part."

"A suit isn't good enough?"

"Not a human one."

BROOKE SNIFFED the ladle of water Kerren had handed to her. "I don't understand."

"You drink this, and it allows you to safely pass through the portal."

"The portal itself isn't safe?" she asked.

"The portal is just a portal. The reflecting pool combines with the portal."

She drank the liquid, which was surprisingly sweet, and handed him the scoop. "It doesn't sound like you know exactly how it works."

"I don't," he admitted, filling the scoop again for himself. "But I've used it hundreds of times."

"So, I won't come out on the other side with two heads?"

He laughed and drank, closing his eyes and shivering as he swallowed. "I'll never get used to that chill, though."

"What chill? It tastes like fruity water."

"Hmm. Maybe it's different for you. To me, it's like swallowing ice, and it runs through my veins."

She arched a brow. That didn't seem pleasant. She took a step towards the portal, heart pounding and skin tingling with anticipation. It looked like an arch, the fancy type used for outdoor weddings. Lush purple blossoms hung from a vine wrapping tightly around it, like a cross between a lily and an orchid. It was aurleis, a flower of Sidera Luminis, Kerren had explained, one cultivated specifically by the royal bloodline.

"I can't believe the Landsgate is literally a gateway," she breathed. "The Landsgate Faerriot. I had no idea, and I know just about everything about this city."

"Yeah," he said, standing beside her and looking at the arch. "They keep the secret well. To anyone else looking at this roof, it's just like any other. The gate cloaks itself and everything around it."

"So, we're practically invisible right now?"

He nodded.

"I'm nervous," she admitted aloud. "And I still keep going back and forth between excited and a little pissed."

He snorted. "Welcome to my life growing up."

"Meaning?"

"Long story," he muttered. Reaching out, he took her hand. "You may feel a bit… I believe the human term is 'jet-lagged,' once the trip is done."

"Yay," she said sarcastically under her breath.

She adjusted her grip on him, lacing their fingers and squeezing him tight. The one thing she was certain of was that he'd take care of her, though she wasn't sure how she had such confidence in it. Sure, they'd just met, and yes it wasn't like her to get naked on a first date—if what they had even counted as a date—but Kerren wasn't like any guy she'd ever met.

And somehow, that was a little scarier than stepping through a gateway to another world.

Holding her breath, she walked forward, Kerren's hand placed comfortingly on the small of her back. For a moment she seemed to fall, and her muscles tensed to catch herself and land. Then she was standing in the middle of an open field, green blades of wispy grass tickling her ankles.

She took a step forward, heels sinking into soft dirt. In the distance, she saw trees and colorful flowers. Further away were houses, as if they'd landed in a quaint countryside. It wasn't night, as Kerren had predicted, but the sun was low on the pink horizon.

Turning back, she found that the arch was now plain wood and engraved with strange swirling symbols. After a minute, a man walked through it, squinting as if staring into the sun.

"Kerren?"

"Yes?"

Brooke stared. Though the voice was the same, much had changed of his appearance. His skin was still the olive hue but now seemed to have an inner golden glow, accenting his aquiline nose and artist-carved perfect cheekbones and strong jaw. His brown eyes were now green and deep, as if peering through an emerald shifting facets in the sun.

His plain brown hair had transformed to be varying shades of earthy browns and forest greens and was longer, the ends curling around the collar of his shirt.

In a nutshell, he was magnificent.

"Ah. I forgot to mention. The reflecting pool adjusts us to fit in wherever we travel." This is my true appearance."

"Wow," Brooke whispered.

He nodded. "Shocking, I suppose? Does it… upset you?"

She arched a brow. "Upset me? To know that underneath the human playboy you're still a magically sexy duke?"

One side of his mouth twitched into a crooked grin. "Oh. I just assumed a human woman wouldn't find this side of me appealing."

"You're appealing to me all over again," she admitted.

Grinning smugly, he pointed to a path to the left. "Let's make our way, then." He crooked his elbow and she took it. "Welcome to Sidera Luminis, by the way."

BROOKE CHEWED her lip anxiously as she walked beside Kerren. Since she'd spent the night with him, she only had the same dress she'd worn the day before. It was one of her favorites, but it seemed a bold choice for the current occasion.

She hadn't thought much of it before, but now she guessed that her clothing was like a beacon screaming '*Hi! I'm a human!*'

They passed a group of women who were chatting in the street. The women wore long flowing dresses of simple cuts, but there was something special about the fabric, as if it shifted colors. Teal became gold then soft petal pink.

Something she'd noticed was how often faces turned to them and after appraising Brooke seemed to subtly acknowledge Kerren.

"Where are we, exactly?" she asked Kerren.

"My province," he replied. "Weylan Barrows. Though, once I return to Earth, it will be absorbed into the kingdom. Or perhaps they'll pass it to someone else."

"When you say 'yours' you mean…"

"I mean that it is actually mine, yes. I inherited this land and my title from my mother."

Trying not to trip from the thought of owning an entire province, Brooke glanced to him. "Then why wouldn't she get it back?"

"She doesn't want it. My mother is sweet but flighty. The politics and responsibilities of caring for a people were never meant to be her lot in life."

"Oh."

"She's traveling right now, anyhow. She has a direct lineage to the aspect of… I think the best way to describe it would be "flowering." It gives her a talent for helping areas that struggle to sustain plant life."

That probably explained his intimate knowledge of his own planet's foliage. Brooke tried to imagine Kerren's mother, but it was difficult to not see her as a winged woman, touching things and making them grow. Granted, she hadn't seen any wings on anyone so far. A few gently pointed ears and strange (to her) shades of skin and hair, but nothing like she'd expected.

She was thinking Tinkerbell and met nothing of the sort.

"I'll change quickly, then we'll head to the palace. It's not far. We travel using a bridge… it's similar to the portal, but it's really just a connection hub."

"Right," she said, confused.

"Maybe it's better if you don't think about it too much," he admitted. "I have to imagine that magic must be overwhelming to someone accustomed to science."

Chuckling, she shook her head. "It's not that. Or not that exactly. I'm still reeling from even being here. And honestly, I'm still wondering why you'd leave. Everything is gorgeous, and you're right about it feeling lighter somehow. The air is just refreshing and uplifting. My brain is stressing, but my body has never felt better."

"I'm glad you like it." He pulled her to a stop at the beginning of a stone walkway and gestured to the massive ivy-covered mansion at the end. "Welcome to my home."

CHAPTER 6

Kerren did his best to appear calm around Brooke, but inside there was nothing but panic flowing through his veins. Humans were so rarely called to appear for the King and Queen, it had never before happened in his lifetime.

Usually, it had to do with crimes against the court—but Brooke had done no such thing. Whatever Artur and Catriona had in mind, it was a mystery.

Kerren would be lying if he acted as if it wasn't entertaining to have the opportunity to show Brooke the fae world. She'd been fascinated by every little detail he'd shared, and if any human deserved to see it for themselves, it was her.

He adjusted his dark russet formal coat one last time in the mirror, brushing his fingertips over the embroidered edge of the collar that designated him as the protector of Weylan Barrows. It was a hollow title, really. Since the wars had ended centuries before he was even born, he'd never had to protect anything.

He owned the land, he respected the people, that was it. Being away had been nice, but since he'd stepped foot into his house he'd immediately begun to wonder what unforeseen consequences could come of him leaving.

Just because he didn't think he mattered individually as a leader, didn't make it accurate.

Stepping out of his room, he searched for Brooke. The amazement in her eyes had been like a bright light, and he'd welcomed her to explore.

He found her in the library, staring at the expanse of silk-bound books.

"This is breathtaking," she said, turning to him.

"You would be drawn to the section that details fae history, of course," he pointed out, making note of where she stood.

She ran her hands along the wooden ledge of the nearest shelf. "I can't read them, though."

"The language of the fae," he explained. "But it's easier for humans to learn than for us."

"How so?"

He smirked. "How do you think?"

"Magic?"

He nodded and walked to her. She looked him over with a soft expression, one he recognized.

"You like this, don't you?"

"Everything is just… wow." Her hands landed on his coat and she bit her lower lip. "You look good. Very important and formal."

"And you look stunning."

Pink bloomed on her cheeks and she looked away. "I feel out of place."

"You're not. There are other humans here. Some from Earth, some from places quite similar," he reassured her.

"No, I mean in this house. With you. I guess I didn't

consider it when we met, because I was told that once you were on Earth long enough, you'd no longer be royalty. You'd just be another guy, albeit ridiculously rich. And to be fair, I've never seemed to get along with the wealthy. But here, this is you and your life, and it's an entire world of wow."

He cupped her jaw and tilted her face up to look at him. "This isn't my life. This is my past." He combed through her long ruby hair. "It's nothing to feel slighted by."

She leaned into his hand, eyes closed. He wanted to kiss her but knew where that would lead, and they didn't have time for it. The moment they'd arrived on Sidera Luminis, word would have spread. They were expected elsewhere.

As much as he wanted to throw Brooke onto his bed, they needed to hurry and get to the bottom of her summoning.

TWO TALL FAE men stood guard at the entrance to the throne room where Brooke would stand before the court.

"You may head in," one of them announced the moment they came close.

Kerren took a deep breath and drew his shoulders back. Brooke did the same, then stepped forward, allowing the guards to open the doors before her.

Kerren followed a few steps behind. He had not been summoned, and was in attendance only in support of her, after all, but he wasn't going to sit off to the side and leave her alone.

Brooke's shoes made loud, echoing taps across the ivory marble floor, and she stopped at the engraved emblem at the center of the room as he'd advised her to.

He quickly scanned the room, noting that almost every seat was filled with royal bloods. His heart raced at the ominous sign. The heads of crown-related houses rarely sat for minor matters. For them to be here meant something big had occurred.

King Artur shared a look with his wife, who offered a wide smile to Brooke. Artur scratched his thick beard, so dark it looked black at a distance. Artur was half forest element, a rare fae, and he looked the part. Rugged and woodsy, even in his formal tunic. The crown couldn't hide his primal aura. His brown eyes were turned to his wife, and he whispered.

Seeming to ignore her husband's whispers, Catriona studied Brooke with open admiration. She smoothed a hand over the tightly woven complex braids of gold and russet hair that held up her crown, clearly envying Brooke's long and loose style.

Catriona's bright green eyes sparkled, putting Kerren at immediate ease. Though a descendant of a line of fae warriors, she was built small and delicate. Still, Kerren knew that Catriona was capable of laying down the law when needed, and he was thankful that unless her mood was deceiving, there would be no punishments tonight.

"Welcome, dear," Catriona said loudly.

"Oh… thank you for the summ—invite." Brooke dipped into a wobbly curtsey, which made the Queen's smile grow.

Already, there was the gentle rumble of whispered chatter through the room, and Kerren knew why. Though there was a subtle tremble to Brooke, she stood tall and confident. Even not knowing the purpose of this meeting, she revealed no fear and only a hint of anxiousness.

She was behaving the opposite of how many humans new to Sidera Luminis behaved, and the fae responded with interest.

"We only have a few questions," the Queen explained.

"Humans rarely appreciate the nuances of formality, so we will make this 'painless' as they say."

Brooke nodded.

"How familiar are you with the history of Sidera Luminis?" she asked.

"Not at all familiar, your majesty."

"How did you learn of the fae and this world?"

Brooke's head tilted slightly. "I knew the fae existed, but I only really learned of Sidera Luminis within the last week, when I was asked to be Duke Kerren's guide."

"And how much were you told of the Duke and us?" Artur asked.

"I was told only the basic facts. That the Duke had decided to move to our world, and that our city was a fair match for him. I didn't pry into his business, if that's what you mean."

Catriona crossed her legs and gave her husband a look.

"How dangerous is your city?" he asked.

"I'm not sure… I suppose not very? Our crime rate is about average, if not below that," she replied carefully.

"Did you prepare for these dangers when you decided to offer your services?" Catriona asked.

Kerren stepped forward to Brooke's side, gently touching her elbow as she frowned and seemed to be flustered at the question.

"Guide is not her official position in the human world," he pointed out. "She isn't responsible for the safety of each human, nor could she possibly be expected to account for them."

Artur cleared his throat and leveled a stare at Kerren. "That's not what we asked. We are aware of Ms. Donovan's position in her world."

"Please answer," Catriona pressed.

Brooke shook her head. "I didn't think my world would

be a danger, in honesty. Many of us live our entire lives without being grievously harmed. I certainly didn't place him in danger, though. I could share my itinerary for the week." She shifted on her feet and glanced to Kerren. "No war zones or base jumping," she joked.

The King and Queen didn't appear entertained but were silent for a moment. Brooke's words stirred an idea in Kerren's mind, like a memory he couldn't grasp. There was something he should understand, but it escaped him.

The Queen looked to her right and made a slight gesture with her hand. Vevina came forward and judging by the flame-like flicker of her hair, she was in a flustered mood.

"Vevina of the house Freagh, please tell the court what you witnessed on Earth."

Vevina's eyes were glued to the floor, as if avoiding Kerren altogether. "I, Vevina of the house Freagh, loyal servant to the family and lands of Kerren of Weylan Barrows, witnessed this human, Brooke Donovan, save the life of His Grace."

Everything clicked, and Kerren swore under his breath. Vevina had invoked a human right, even though Brooke had no idea she had access to it.

"It's not proven that I was in mortal danger," he announced. "I very well may have just been injured."

Artur peered at Brooke. "How many humans die from being hit by cars?"

"I have no idea."

"Do they often survive?"

"I... I really can't say. I've never met a person who was hit by a car."

"There would be a repository of information," Kerren pointed out. "I'm sure I wouldn't have died."

"I don't know, Kerren. They were moving so fast..." Brooke said honestly.

He groaned.

"Vevina?" Catriona asked.

Vevina gnawed her lip and raised her head to face the Queen. "Ms. Donovan is correct. From what I can tell, the odds of a person surviving impact of a car on that road, given the speed of travel, it would be around five percent."

Kerren's heart flipped, both from hearing that he'd been closer to death than he was willing to accept and because Vevina had solidly sealed her case. He couldn't imagine her goal, but she had single-handedly redirected Brooke's life.

Brooke took his hand, staring into his eyes. "But you didn't get hurt. That's the point, right?"

He nodded. She was clueless.

The King and Queen stood.

"I can't even remember the last time we had such wondrous news," the Queen announced gleefully. "By the right of the court, and in the act of saving the life of noble blood, Brooke Donovan is hereby indoctrinated into the court. The newest Lady of Weylan Barrows." She clapped her hands together. "And of course, the official ceremony will be in... hmm. Let's say three days."

"Excuse me?" Brooke whispered. "I'm what?"

Kerren couldn't speak, his jaw clenched so tight it hurt. He watched Vevina slide from the room like a snake. After everything he'd been through, her treachery was the worst. He'd finally had what he wanted—a new beginning, a perfect woman in his arms—and now he'd have nothing.

The room filled with overlapping conversations, no longer whispers but now a steady roar. Confusion spread across Brooke's brows and she tugged Kerren's coat.

"I'll explain," he promised. "We should leave."

"Is something wrong? It didn't sound like bad news," she pressed. "I'm a member of the court? How? As a human?"

"I'll explain," he repeated, taking her hand.

He led her away, through scattered applause and excited congratulations. Of course it was wonderful news to them. The Pure fae court loved humans who somehow rose above the rest.

Brooke would be the topic of discussion for the next decade.

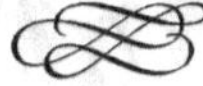

CHAPTER 7

Kerren had been quiet on the way back to his home, but it spoke volumes. He was angry, furious even, and Brooke had no idea why.

She asked questions, tried to speak to him, but nothing got through. He was a wall, and she wasn't breaking through.

On the surface, she understood the Queen's words. She, Brooke, was now a member of the fae court. But what that meant was a mystery. Even more questionable was Kerren's reaction. Why did it seem like he hated the world right now?

She followed him through his home, a winding maze that eventually led to the kitchen. He pulled down two glasses and produced a bottle of what she assumed was wine from one of the cupboards.

Though the kitchen appeared modern at first glance, there was no fridge or stove or oven. Instead, a raised marble inlaid fireplace sat against the wall. There were shelves of strange jars and pots, and baskets of fruits and vegetables. Some she recognized, but mostly things that were clearly fae in origin.

"I'm sorry," he said, pouring a dark amber liquid into each

glass. "If I had suspected, perhaps I could have circumvented things."

She watched him slide the glass across the counter towards her and sigh heavily. He spoke as if he grieved, and she still didn't understand.

"Are you going to explain now?" she asked.

He pinched the bridge of his nose and squeezed his eyes shut. After a moment he took a sip of his wine, and after swallowing he leaned forward.

"You are now a memb—"

"I heard that. What does it mean?" she interrupted.

"It means that you, as a human and non-royal blood, are now required to uphold the tenets of the station. Primarily, it means that when I welcomed you to Sidera Luminis, I may as well have said 'Welcome home,' because that's what this is."

She fingered the stem of her glass, certain that she misunderstood. "I have a home. On Earth. I have a tiny apartment that I can barely afford, but I love it."

"I'm sure you'll be gifted a modest estate now," he said dryly.

A heavy weight sunk into her stomach. "What about my life? My job?"

"Of the particulars—I don't know. I just know you'll be taken care of."

She fell into the stool beside her and took a deep sip of the strange wine. It was bittersweet and thicker than it appeared, but she pushed aside her curiosity. There were larger matters at hand.

"You aren't forced to stay here," she reasoned.

"That's different. Humans indoctrinated into the court don't have a choice—or rather, the fae can't imagine a human not choosing life as fae nobility over a normal human existence."

She took a deep breath, trying to tamp down the rising

panic by tackling her anxiety with reason. One thing she hated about her life was predictability. She wanted to travel and had always dreamed of moving to a new city and meeting new people. In a way, she could look at this as an opportunity.

Except it wasn't her choice.

Even if the prospect was exhilarating, there was a dark undertone. She'd never know if she was meant for something else. Her future was partially out of her hands. She wouldn't miss her job, or her boss, or her tiny apartment—which she'd lied about loving. But she would miss that everything she had, she'd gotten on her own.

She took another drink and regarded Kerren's continuing scowl. For a moment she felt a hint of solace, but it fell away. Kerren didn't want to live on Sidera Luminis, and it was unlikely that he'd stay around just to spend more time with her.

Their time together had been fleeting, but she'd hoped it was leading somewhere.

"Will you stick around long enough for the ceremony?" she asked sadly.

"Of course," he said simply.

That was that. No note of anything more. Theirs was one magical night and nothing else.

She swirled her glass, holding it up and staring at it through the light. "I know why I'm torn between running and jumping for joy, but what about you? You seem ready to fight someone."

"I feel betrayed," he admitted.

"Betrayed? How? I'm the one who just got dragged into a new society."

He shrugged. "Vevina..." his voice trailed off and he sighed. "I can't believe she'd do this to me—I mean, to you."

Brooke narrowed her eyes at him. "She was only doing

what she had to, wasn't she?"

"No. She didn't have to tell anyone about what happened. It's a technicality. Had I signed over my land and title before leaving, this wouldn't be an issue. But because I was undecided, and wanted my province to be handled organically, it meant I was—or rather still am—fae nobility." He growled into his glass and tilted his head back, polishing off his drink. "To drag you into this was unfair."

"I don't understand."

He didn't say anything, and Brooke hated feeling like there was something missing from his explanation. Nothing he said explained Vevina's actions. He was acting as if it had everything to do with him when she was the only one affected.

"How is it unfair to you?" she pressed.

Pouring himself another half-glass, he eyed her. "My actions have snowballed and taken you under."

It seemed a flimsy argument, but perhaps he had guilt issues, even if she didn't blame him at all for what had unfolded.

"As I said, I'm sorry," he repeated, appearing hellbent on allowing the unnecessary self-blame to bring him under.

Reaching out, she took his wrist and stopped him from downing his wine.

"On the bright side, you get to show me around. I want the full tour. What do you think my average day would entail here?" She laughed softly, trying to hide the tears that brimmed upon thinking of her new life. "I mean, are there jobs? Does anyone need a mediocre purchasing agent with three years in industrial supply?"

He put down his glass and took hers away as well. "There are opportunities you've probably never dreamt of, and I highly doubt you're capable of being mediocre at anything." He pulled her from the stool and led her to the nearest window, standing behind her. "Point out anything in the distance and I'll take you there. Or just tell me what you want to see. Anything that sparks your curiosity."

Leaning back, she pressed her back against the sturdy wall of his chest. She closed her eyes, hoping her request wasn't too forward.

"Your bedroom," she whispered.

His arms circled her, and he bent to her ear. "Are you sure?"

"Take my mind off it all, Kerren. Right now, you're the only thing I understand."

Sweeping her hair to the side, he kissed her neck, then growled softly. "We need to get you some dresses that don't require pliers and perfect vision to remove."

BROOKE LAY in the center of Kerren's wondrous canopy bed, waiting for him to return. He'd stripped her dress off and stared at her body while mumbling to himself, then promised he'd be right back. She'd removed her bra and settled into the plush mattress, eager to see what he had in mind.

The bedroom was decorated in the same manner of the rest of his home. Each piece of furniture looked antique and expensive. The posts of the bed were a golden wood, polished to a smooth sheen and engraved with intricate vines. The sheets were mellow tan and buttery soft against her skin. Diaphanous curtains fell on each side of the bed, tied back with golden ropes.

Before the bed was a fluffy hunter green rug, and she'd had naughty thoughts of rolling around on it with Kerren, but the bed had called to her.

It was nearly twice the size of her bed at home, and even more comfortable than it looked, which hardly seemed fair.

"Here," Kerren said, entering the room.

He'd removed his coat and shirt, and wore only his russet formal pants, which seemed to be the softest brushed leather in all of existence. Climbing beside her on the bed, he set down a bowl.

"What did you bring me?" she asked rising on her elbows.

"You mentioned you had a sweet tooth. I thought these would be nice… and fun." He produced a fruit, which seemed like a large, petal pink strawberry. "Open."

She opened her mouth and nibbled the faux strawberry. The seeds were larger and more noticeable and burst in her mouth with a tangy surprise. The fruit itself was like biting into heaven, sweet and light. The flesh seemed to melt in her mouth like cotton candy.

She moaned and took another bite, finishing it off to the stem. "This is incredible," she purred. "What is it?"

"I'm sure you could guess, but it's related to the strawberries of Earth. We can't grow those exactly—they require acidic soil, whatever that is—"

"Kerren."

He laughed and grabbed another pink berry. "We call them Fenberries. I thought you would like them."

She took a bite of the offered berry and sighed as the flavors exploded over her tongue. "Mmmm. I love them. Definitely enough for my sweet cravings."

He scooted close and licked her bottom lip. "You've given me a sweet tooth," he commented. "Your pussy has me addicted."

Heat flooded her cheeks and her panties grew damp at his words. "You're ridiculous."

He sucked her lip into his mouth and she gradually relented. His tongue swept across hers as they kissed, sending sparks of fire through her bloodstream. He pulled away and licked down her neck while he fed her the remainder of the berry.

Tangling her fingers in his thick multi-hued hair, she begged under her breath. She couldn't remember ever wanting a man the way she wanted Kerren. And maybe, more importantly, she'd never met a man who seemed to want her with such equal passion.

His ravenous mouth devoured her skin, nipping at her breasts with teasing teeth. He took another berry by the stem and dragged the chilled fruit across her already erect nipples. The bumps of pronounced seeds were an odd sensation, one he followed with his tongue, replacing cool and hard with warm and wet.

Under normal circumstances, Brooke didn't enjoy sex without commitment, but normal had left the building. Right now, she needed Kerren. He touched her with a familiarity that made no sense given their short acquaintance but gave her exactly the comfort she needed.

Scooting down her body, he guided the berry in a winding path down her stomach, circled it around her navel, and traveled lower still. He paused at her underwear.

"Do you really need these?" he asked fingering the delicate fabric.

"Not now."

He gripped the black lace and ripped it from her body, the sudden sting flashing across her skin.

"I didn't mean I'd never need them again," she gasped. It was, after all, the only pair she had with her.

"My mistake," he said with a grin. "Accept my apologies?"

His head dove down, kissing where her thighs met and making her breath catch. He nudged her legs open and hissed in approval.

"Perfect," he whispered in appreciation.

She bit her cheek and watched him. The cool textured skin of the berry trailed on her inner thigh in sweeping up and down motions, teasing her. Her pussy was wet and aching for his attention, and each second that he ignored it made her wild.

"You're driving me crazy," she whined.

"Just lay back and close your eyes."

She did as told. Before she could wonder what he was up to, he'd slid something cool and bumpy along her folds, using it to part her open. She gripped the sheets and kept her eyes squeezed shut as the strange sensation became clear.

He dipped the berry into her wet slit and teased her entrance. Her legs shook with anticipation as he twisted and eased it in and out, barely entering her but going far enough to make her salivate. The teasing whipped her nerves into a frenzy.

The firm flesh of fruit was replaced by warmth, his tongue licking her wet slit. He moaned against her skin as he glided the berry across her clit, rubbing the seeded surface across her sensitive bud as his tongue dived in and out of her dripping wet pussy.

"Kerren," she begged. "Please, I need you inside me."

His tongue flattened and lapped over her from entrance to clit, as if he would lick up every drop of her. She raised up on her elbow to see him. Digging her hand through his thick waves, she shuddered. The way he looked up at her, hunger blatant in his eyes, floored her. He gave her pussy another long, deliberate lick then popped the berry into his mouth.

While she stared, he stepped off the bed to remove his pants. They laced in the front, and though he wasn't trying to put on a show, she was nearly excited enough to clap. His erection sprang free, causing her mouth to water.

He climbed up her body and kissed her. The sweet and tangy juice of the berry, mingled with her own fresh flavor laced his tongue, and she swallowed it all. The head of his cock nestled against her folds, poised to enter, and he rocked his hips so that he glided in her arousal.

"I love the way you taste," he whispered against her mouth.

One quick thrust and he slid inside her, taking her breath away. He was thick and smooth, and she felt full nearly to the point of him being too much. He groaned and pressed against her, working his way deeper. She hadn't guessed he wasn't all the way in yet, and that realization made her head spin.

"You're so tight," he said through clenched teeth.

She nodded and dug her fingertips into his back, speechless. His every shift and movement stretched her open for him until finally, he'd buried himself completely.

He kissed her mouth and chin, then growled into her ear, "Perfect fit."

"Oh, fuck," she murmured.

"That's the plan."

He pulled himself out half-way then rammed back in, shaking her entire body with the force of his action and making her eyes roll back in pleasure.

"Like this? Or is slower more your style?" he asked. "You said you liked it hard…"

It took her a moment to find words, as if she'd devolved into mute puddle of lust. "Yes," she panted. "Please, more like that."

He grinned, and she braced himself as he pistoned in and out of her, quick and hard, like a beast fueled by primal need. She enjoyed sex of just about any flavor, but tonight this was exactly what she needed—raw, mind-numbing fucking.

The bed shook, and she held onto him, thighs pressed to his sides, nails scraping his back and arms.

"I want to feel you squeezing my cock when you finish," he said breathing heavily.

"Yes," she promised.

She would never have guessed this side of him existed. Perhaps he wasn't the most rigid or cold man, but he was nobility. She thought for certain they were going to have sex in the most proper way possible—whatever that may have been.

Instead, she was crying out in pleasure while he did his best to push into her so roughly it seemed he meant to go through her. Her breathing could hardly keep up, and her pounding heartbeat seemed to echo off the walls.

Pleasure built up like a coil, braced to explode each time he slammed home and pressed his pelvis to her clit. The muscles of his back rippled beneath her frantically exploring hands, as she gave in and let go.

Her body quivered beneath him and she gasped as if stealing her last breath. Waves of bliss enveloped her and flowed through her, turning her bones liquid. Her inner walls spasmed as he curled his body to hers and shoved deeper, prolonging her orgasm.

Holding her tight he exhaled against the crook of her neck. His cock throbbed within her, spilling his seed.

She sought his mouth, turning her face for a kiss. A soft green glow caught her attention, and the haze around her mind lifted enough to register the source. His emerald eyes were lit like a strange fire, and she became lost in them.

Reality came crashing forward. There was no way she could walk away from him as if he were a one-night stand. Her heart ached as her thoughts spun through wild schemes. She couldn't stay, or he couldn't go. They needed more time.

CHAPTER 8

Kerren didn't normally eat breakfast, but the previous night's activities had made him awaken ravenous. He dumped berries onto two bowls of spiced porridge and grabbed several sweet rolls.

He'd mostly emptied his home of food since he was leaving, and Vevina was supposed to take care of the rest, but instead, she'd restocked. While he was grateful for this, she was still a traitor.

In addition to the food, he'd found a suitcase full of dresses in the living room, and he knew they had to be from Brooke's personal wardrobe, being of the fit and fabric not found on Sidera Luminis. Meaning that on top of her other offense, she'd apparently broken into Brooke's home.

He dragged the wheeled luggage up the stairs along with the tray of food he'd prepared. He found Brooke in bed, sitting up but staring out the window.

"Are you hungry?"

She looked over and smiled as he set the tray down. "I'm starving."

"It's not a typical breakfast. We don't have bacon and eggs here," he said, as she crawled towards the food.

"I can't believe I'm going to live in a world without bacon," she groaned, pouting. "Bacon is life."

He tore a roll in half, trying not to stare at her bare breasts glowing in the sunlight that seeped into the room. "The hotel guide mentioned it, and it suggested that it was part of the typical American breakfast. Bacon, eggs, pancakes."

"That sounds delicious," she said digging her spoon into the porridge. "But this looks and smells amazing, so I'm not complaining."

Brooke took a bite and moaned. Kerren wasn't sure if it was an Earth habit, a woman habit, or just her own idiosyncrasy that led her to make such tantalizing sounds when she ate, but he loved it all the same.

It made him want to track down whatever bacon was, just to witness her reaction.

"I thought we could walk around today, just see what catches your eye," he said changing the subject.

She nodded and bit into a piece of sweet bread. Her eyes closed and she bounced slightly, as if overwhelmed by the taste of it.

"Does everything here taste so phenomenal," she asked finally.

He laughed. "My opinion would be biased, but I'd say probably."

She tore the bread apart and scooped it through the porridge. "It's the little things that make life grand."

"I'd agree. But as far as the other things, Vevina brought some of your personal items."

She rocked to the side and eyed the luggage. "I thought that suitcase looked familiar. Another show of fae privilege? Stealing?"

He didn't bother trying to defend his assistant's actions. Just thinking about Vevina plotting such a scheme boiled his blood.

"I hope she packed underwear," Brooke said slyly.

Just like that, his heated blood was redistributing itself. He'd felt a moment of foolishness after tearing her clothing, but in retrospect, she hadn't seemed all that upset.

"Kerren?"

He looked up and found her watching him with an odd expression of caution. "Yes?"

"Do you think I'll fit in? Will it work?"

"Of course. The fae will love you."

"But I'm human, and suddenly I'm… noble, I guess? It sounds like resentment and hostility waiting to happen." She glanced down at her bowl, stirring her food slowly.

Reaching out, he lifted her chin. "It's not like that. I'd be lying if I said there weren't fae who looked down on most humans. And yes, some won't be impressed by a human in the court."

She frowned.

"But," he continued, "You saw how the majority reacted to the announcement. Excited. Humans have a somewhat novel appeal, and most of them come from planets less modernized than your Earth."

"I'm entertaining?" she asked with distaste in her voice.

"Not in the way you assume." He dragged a hand through his hair and tried to explain. "Most humans either stumble upon Sidera Luminis accidentally or are pitied and invited to come and live. They're claimed, which is far from being noble."

"Claimed?"

"It doesn't sound good, but it's just how it goes. Claiming can be like adopting or like hiring a servant. It all depends on the circumstances. A family may step forward and welcome them in, or they take employment. By becoming connected to fae they gain standard rights. They even marry fae, though it's rare," he reasoned. "My point, though, is that humans are usually coming from poverty or are completely downtrodden. That's not you. You're proud and poised. Certain of yourself. You aren't looking at a life on Sidera Luminis as an escape from anything, and that places you on a different level entirely."

She stared at him, then looked down at her food again.

"It's meant to be a compliment," he pointed out.

"I get that, sort of. Sorry but now I'm wondering how one goes about stumbling onto a new planet by accident," she admitted sheepishly.

He chuckled softly. "Some of the demifae can conjure portals. Their portals are intuitive and occasionally call to those you may consider lost souls. Not physically lost, but otherwise adrift. If they end up here, however, it was meant to be. No human who has fallen through a random portal has regretted it."

"But doesn't it insult the court that I'm not here of my own free will? I didn't fall through a portal, I was summoned and now I have no choice."

"They can't fathom you not wanting to be a part of it. Literally, the possibility will not make sense."

"But you understand," she said softly.

"Because I've been trying to get away for half of my life. Blame my mom. I must have inherited her wanderlust. Only my father kept her here. After he gambled his way into a life in prison, she started traveling and I followed suit."

"What? Prison?"

He bit his tongue. Spilling that snippet of truth surprised him, as well. He didn't like to talk about his father. Shrugging, he gave a crooked grin to hide his shame.

"My father wasn't fond of me. As I got older he seemed to

care less about me, and the more my mother doted on me, the less time he spent at home. He gambled and got in trouble, enough that the authorities stepped in took him away. We're expected to act with a certain level of decorum, and he didn't have it. As I said before, restrictions."

"He was jailed for being… inappropriate to his title?"

"Maybe." Kerren furrowed his brow, admitting something he'd hidden his entire life. "I think he was abusing my mother."

Brooke took a deep breath.

"Mother never said anything, but it was like something in the air. Sinister. Artur has been known to look the other way at minor offenses, but something about my father made him lay down punishment. Furthermore, my father's actions should have thrown shame on all of us, yet my mother retained this home and her title."

"I had no idea," Brooke whispered. "I'm sorry to have brought it up, Kerren."

"No, it's fine. Maybe it's a good thing to know. To see the fairer side of the King you'll be serving. I didn't understand when I was younger, but time has made me see. The way my mother would keep her distance at times, how her smile would become fake when we'd sit at dinner. I believe that Artur hid the extent of my father's true crimes so that there would be no stigma on my mother and me. There are worse men that have ruled the Pure court."

Brooke placed her hand over Kerren's and squeezed it gently. He'd never spoken to a soul about the dark mystery around his childhood. His mother was too content now for him to bring it up without feeling guilty, and to the rest of Sidera Luminis, his father was simply a rowdy and unworthy scoundrel.

Only Brooke placed him at such ease that deep secrets could spill forth without causing pain. If any human deserved to be placed on a pedestal and admired by the fae, it was her.

KERREN WAITED downstairs while Brooke bathed and got dressed, killing time by sprinkling the flowers in his back-yard with honey crystals. Come night, the pixies would find the sweet treat and turn his garden into a demifae party. It was the type of magical treat that would hopefully remove the sting from Brooke's fate.

He wanted her to focus on the positives.

Dusting off his hands, he went back inside and found Brooke descending the stairs. Her luxurious red tresses were curled and spilling over one shoulder, contrasting against her pale skin. She wore a cream sleeveless blouse with a ruffled bow in the front, tucked into a fitted, black and white pinstripe skirt.

Black heels completed the look, but she held a pair of flats in her hand.

"You said walk, and I'm not sure if where we're going is paved or what," she said waving the shoes. "I'm still pissed at Vevina but thank goodness she thought to pack options. I guess I have enough for now, until I hit the nearest fae dress store…"

"You look amazing," he said, taking her free hand as she came close. "You know, you don't have to switch to wearing the traditional fae clothing. You could dress like this and I don't think anyone would complain. Or at least, certainly not the men… and perhaps a third of the women."

Pink bloomed on her cheeks. "Maybe. It may be easier to just wear what I'm used to. Fae women tend to be… smaller, from what I've seen. I don't want to have to wear curtains or something."

He chuckled. "Fae come in all sizes. If you want traditional gowns, you'll have them. Why on Earth would you wear curtains?"

"Hmm. Pop culture reference." She held up her shoes. "So?"

"Heels are fine unless they hurt your feet. I just want you to be comfortable."

She pursed her lips and appeared to be thinking deeply on the subject. "I think I'll stay the way I am for now. Don't ask me why, but I think I need the boost."

"What boost?"

"It's probably silly to you, but between making me taller and making my legs look incredible, the heels are helping me feel like myself. And every little bit helps right now, because I just took a bath in a magical tub that heated the water and added perfume and bubbles without me even lifting a finger."

He scratched his head. "Oh. Some things will take a lot of getting used to, I suppose."

"Understatement of the year," she whispered.

After setting her shoes down in a corner, she reached into a hidden pocket of her skirt and held out a paper. "By the way, this floated in through the window while I was bathing. It's in your language. And another by the way, the window was closed, and it went through the glass."

He arched a brow and took the slip of paper, reading it and translating it aloud. "The Queen requests your presence for high tea to discuss your future station and make arrangements." He glanced up at her. "That's quite the honor. You had to have made an impression to be invited for tea. I'm a duke and I've never had tea with her."

She sighed softly. "What are the odds that I can negotiate out of my future station?"

"Do you really want to?"

She cast a glance out the window. "I don't know."

"I have something to show you." He held out his arm and she took it. "We've got time before I need to escort you to the Queen's garden.

"Lead the way."

CHAPTER 9

BROOKE

*B*rooke stared up at a magnificent alabaster statue of a fae queen, sword held skyward, expression defiant. The sculptor had captured such detail that every strand of her tousled hair seemed significant, and the embroidered edge of her dress looked like stitching that had been coated in perfect plaster.

"Brea was a champion in the last battle for peace," Kerren said. He gestured to the plaque on her pedestal, words in his language which she couldn't read. "Also, our only Queen to never choose a partner."

"That happens? No king?"

"They always rule jointly, and it wasn't a time where she felt she could trust anyone. A fair assessment, truly. After the peace accords were signed, her general poisoned her."

Brooke's jaw dropped. "You're kidding. Her general? Isn't that the one person she should've been able to count on?"

"That was why he poisoned her, or at least that was his claim. He loved her, and though she loved him in return, she wouldn't marry and make him king. She kept secrets from him until the end. She placed the safety of the future of the Pure court over her own heart."

"That doesn't make sense. If he loved her, he wouldn't kill her."

Kerren shrugged. "We all handle emotions differently. His love became obsession, madness. He feared her love wasn't true since she wouldn't trust him. Instead of walking away, he killed her, confessed, and killed himself."

"I hope he doesn't have a statue," Brooke said horrified.

"No. Certainly not. Though Brea helped establish peace, the first thing that happened afterward was a succession argument. She had no husband and no direct heir. Eventually, the council appealed to the aspects for help." Kerren placed a hand on the small of Brooke's back and guided her to a large group monument. "The aspects are the oldest fae. They birthed deities. Choosing a ruler for the Pure court was the last formal decision they made before retiring into the fade."

"There's a lot I didn't understand about what you just said," Brooke admitted. "Aspects. Deities. The fade?"

"Hmm. But you want to learn, don't you?" he asked, eyes glittering.

She grinned. Of course she did. "I brought you to a garden in the middle of the city to give you a place to feel at home. You brought me to the center of your peoples' history."

"Does it help? Did it work?"

Nodding, she laced her fingers with his and shifted her body closer to him. She wanted to hold him. Kiss him. But that would hurt her in the end. Squeezing his hand was as much as she could allow herself. She would enjoy him while it lasted.

"Speaking of history and magic and things I don't understand… why did your eyes glow last night?"

Kerren smirked and glanced around as if he suspected eavesdroppers. They weren't alone, but no one seemed close enough to hear. Then again, maybe the fae had crazy abilities.

"In some moments, my spirit is freer," he said cryptically. "And the eyes are the windows."

She tugged his hand and led him down a path, until they were barely in eyesight of anyone else. "Your spirit is a burning green fire?"

"Of course not."

"Then?" she insisted.

He narrowed his eyes. "It's a secret that isn't really a secret."

"Kerren," she said flatly. "Since when do you play games like this?"

His jaw ticked and once again he looked around. Finally, he sighed and led her to a fence. Waving his hand over the copper bars, a gate appeared, and he guided her through. Another wave of his hand made the gate return to endless fence, and he walked her towards what looked like a massive hedge maze.

"Most fae have abilities. Flight, speed, mind-reading, a wild array. But the most common is shapeshifting," he explained as he walked her into the tall bushes.

"This doesn't sound like a secret."

"Shifting is limited. Some can become small like demifae. Some can become birds or snakes, whatever."

"That's what you are? A shifter?"

His lips quirked into a sad smile. "Of the rarest sort. Unfortunately, the sight of my shifted form tends to cause unwanted attention."

Her curiosity bubbled over, trying to imagine what he could mean. "Keep going."

"The cu sidhe is a beast of the hunt, with lineage tracing

back to the deities of death. A few fae know this is my spirit form, even fewer have seen it. It would be too proud of an action to flaunt it."

"Death and hunting, don't you mean it would be frightening?"

"No. The cu sidhe all took the same side during the last war, so any Pure fae would be envious or awestruck." His eyes started to glow as he spoke. "The form is one of profound respect and heritage."

Brooke came to a stop and looked him over. She couldn't imagine Kerren being anything but the man standing before her. "Can I see it? Your cootchy form?"

He gave her a confused look. "It's not cootchy. It's cu sidhe. Coo. Shee."

"Cu sidhe," she said carefully. "Sorry. But still, can I see it? We're all alone and I promise not to fall to my knees like a crazed fan."

He arched a brow. "I'm not sure promising not to get on your knees for me is incentive."

"You know what I mean." She rolled her eyes playfully. "I'd really appreciate it. It's not fair to tell me you have a spirit form, then leave it up to my imagination."

Without a word, he yanked off his shirt and handed it to her, then stepped out of his boots and pants. As usual, he wore nothing underneath, a habit that absolutely delighted her. By the time he'd kicked his boots out of the way, his eyes were entirely consumed with the green fire she'd seen the night before.

She took a step back, not afraid but unsure of what to expect. He paced for a moment, then his form shimmered. The odor of soot filled the air and a whooshing giant flame encased him for a split-second before dying away and leaving a massive, shaggy, green hound-like creature where Kerren once stood. The glowing emerald eyes stared at her, and she stumbled further back, knees weak from the shock of witnessing his change.

"Kerren?"

He padded to her and circled her, sniffing the air. She reached out tentatively and stroked his head. He whined and shook his coat as he turned away. A strange bald patch decorated his left flank and she tried to make it out. It appeared to be a brand, like a crude twist of vines.

She started to ask about it but changed her mind. The mark could have been intentional, but she couldn't imagine what purpose. More likely it was an old injury.

He walked away, and with another flash of fire was returned to his fae form. He took his shirt from her shaking hands and offered her a smile.

"You may be the only human in the last hundred or so years to have seen a cu sidhe," he commented.

"That's..." She shook her head. "Wow."

"As I said, few know that I have this ability."

"Your secret is safe with me, of course," she promised.

A TALL FAE woman with jet black hair to her knees led Brooke through the winding garden and to a white gazebo in the clearing. Queen Catriona sat waiting, and upon seeing Brooke's approach, held out her hand in a welcoming gesture.

"There you are. I was worried that Kerren had forgotten all protocol. I'm sure most have forgotten when high tea is held."

"Thank you for the invitation, Your Majesty," Brooke said while seating herself across from Catriona. She kept a smile on her face, but inside she was panicking and wondering if there was a certain way to speak to a queen.

"I'm sure you must be excited, as are we all, truly. It's been quite some time since we introduced another human to the court. The last was long before my time," Catriona said.

Her voice had the same gentle accent as Kerren's, something that made each word sound more musical and formal, and her eyes had a familiar warmth in their green depths.

Brooke smoothed her hands nervously over her skirt and admired Catriona's gown. It was like many of the dresses she'd seen on the other fae women, simple in cut and style, except that Catriona's had long draping sleeves embroidered with the same swirling emblem she'd seen on the floor of the throne room.

Catriona lifted the teapot and poured Brooke a small amount, then pushed a tray of various condiments that appeared to be sweeteners like honey. Her sleeves shifted color in the light, from deep violet to olive green and gold.

"What has Kerren explained to you, dear?"

"Not too much. He showed me around the Barrows." Brooke picked a random honey and stirred it into her tea, causing the scent of spices and flowers to waft in the air, tickling her nose. "I had some concern... I have a job and responsibilities on Earth. It's not so easy for a working human to just up and leave," she said carefully.

"Lorelei will take care of that. You should look forward, not back."

"But my job..."

"I'm sure whatever you did on Earth was beneath you," the Queen countered politely.

Brooke straightened in her chair. "What I did on Earth was something I'd earned through arduous work, regardless of how it may appear to the outside world."

"Yes. And Sidera Luminis is in need of such a clever mind as yours. Do you think your talents would go to waste?"

"I've just never been a fan of handouts," Brooke said firmly.

The Queen arched a brow and took a slow sip of her tea. Placing her cup down on its saucer, she pulled a tray of cookies from the side of the table to the center. They looked scrumptious, but Brooke wasn't going to be distracted from her goal.

"Ms. Donovan, I have never been one to tolerate 'hand-outs' and I wonder if perhaps you are taking for granted the debt we owe you. You saved a life."

"Any human would have—" Brooke bit her tongue. "Okay, many humans would have done the same."

"Perhaps. But it was you." Catriona looked Brooke over. "In my long life, I've gotten adept at reading people. You are a firecracker, yes? You are here, arguing with me over something written in fae law. Gutsy."

"I wasn't really arguing, Your Majesty" Brooke offered, worried she'd come across too harsh. Catriona wasn't just any fae, but it was hard to know exactly how blunt she could be.

"Splitting hairs, dear. And speaking of hair, that gorgeous mane of yours is likely to start a new trend, if not your daring fashion," Catriona said with a mischievous grin. She patted her own golden blonde hair, which was braided at the sides and sat in a high bun decorated with tiny gems. "The life you can have here will be far more fascinating than what Earth could have offered, and just by looking at you, it seems this is fate. Don't tell me you didn't hate your job. Don't tell me you didn't wish for something new and exciting to come along."

"That's not the point. I didn't choose this."

"No. You earned it. Isn't that better?"

Brooke's polite smile faltered. Kerren was right. The other fae couldn't comprehend how her 'award' might not be what every human desired.

"I know that look," Catriona said with a sigh. "Free will and all that, yes?"

"Yes," Brooke said enthusiastically.

"If you'd been invited to live on Sidera Luminis, would you have said yes?"

Brooke nodded and stirred her tea some more. She didn't know how to say it to the Queen, but tea was literally not her cup of tea. There was nothing pleasant about drowned dead leaves.

"Probably," she admitted.

"Your entire internal conflict is based on not having a choice. But it looks like the world chose for you, because you weren't going to make an effort to get what you wanted. How long have you stayed with that job of yours, the one you hate?"

"About three years too long," Brooke confessed.

"And the rest of your dreams? How long have you been settling for less than you deserved?"

The words struck too close for Brooke to dodge. She had been squelching her interest in staying in Sidera Luminis because it wasn't her choice, but there was no denying that she could easily make the best of things and be happy.

Except that entire part about Kerren not being in Sidera Luminis much longer.

"Could there be a compromise?"

"That depends. What compromise do you have in mind?"

"Kerren seemed to think you'd just… bestow things on me. A home. A job. I'd like to be involved in seeing what I'd be comfortable with. I'm not exactly used to a life of luxury."

"We can't have our human nobility living in squalor," the

Queen pointed out. "Of course, we could negotiate the details… but I must admit I have a job in mind."

"Which is?"

"Well, I was going to wait bu—"

A large dark form crashed through the nearest hedge and skidded to a stop. Its dark green paws padded around the grass while Brooke stared in horror. She couldn't imagine why Kerren would crash her tea with the Queen, but there was no way he wasn't going to be in serious trouble.

The burn on his flank seemed more pronounced, as if his fur had gotten shorter, but regardless, she wasn't forgetting the cu sidhe form any time soon.

"Kerren," she hissed. "What are you doing?"

"Kerren?" the Queen asked, standing. She scanned the empty courtyard. "I don't see him."

The hound retreated to hide behind the corner of the pavilion, and she heard the roar of a flame burning and instantly.

"I'm sorry. I wasn't informed that my wife would have company," a deep voice said sheepishly.

Brooke looked away at realizing the naked man behind the railing was not Kerren. Catriona clucked her tongue. "Two hundred and he acts like he's fifty."

"Oh, but, you…" Brooke sputtered. "I'm sorry Your Majesty."

"No, no. In this instance, the fault is all mine, and I offer my sincerest apologies," he insisted, appearing beside the Queen. He'd donned a robe and appeared at ease with his informal attire.

"Why were you speaking of Kerren?" Catriona asked.

"The…" Brooke stared at the ground. "The cu sidhe."

"Ah. Yes, Kerren… that's right. I always forget he has the hunter spirit. Not many of us left," the King said with a deep expression. "A symbol of the old days."

"Yes, and I suppose the burn is part of the spirit then. I was worried Kerren had an injury," she said breathing a sigh of relief.

"Burn?" Artur asked curiously.

"The patch… the twist. On your flank. It's just like Kerren's. I thought maybe he'd been in a fight."

Catriona laughed softly. "Oh. Dear, I'm sure you're mistaken. Every shifter carries their clan mark…" she narrowed her eyes at her husband. "Though usually it is kept well hidden. It is a sign of honor, but then again, it singles the individual out."

"There are no wars, Catriona. There is no longer a need to hide the clan ties or royal blessing," he reasoned.

"I'm quite certain Kerren had that same one, though. Is he of your clan?"

Catriona's smile faltered, and she glanced to Artur. "No. Distant cousins on his mother's side, but he should have the mark of the Barrows."

"The Barrows mark is a circle, though. His was that same twist…" Brooke peered off into the distance, trying to recall it again. "Yes, and I thought perhaps it was from a strange magical duel… my imagination can be wild."

"In any case, you're mistaken," Artur said sternly. He turned to Brooke with a serious line to his brow. "If you don't mind, I think high tea may be over."

"Oh…" Brooke glanced at her untouched drink. She had come close to forcing it down, so she wasn't sad about that, but she still had more questions for the Queen.

"We'll reschedule," the Queen said, glancing at her husband.

"Of course," Brooke said, rising from her seat. "Thank you for having me, Your Majesties."

The same maid from earlier appeared out of nowhere and

gestured for Brooke to follow her. As she walked beside the quiet fae, she tried to recall Kerren's form again.

She'd seen the vines, but perhaps they were right. His fur was long and shaggy. Maybe it had been parted oddly in that spot. There was no other explanation.

93

CHAPTER 10

KERREN

$\mathcal{K}$erren sat at his kitchen table, bent over the cold sandwich he'd made for lunch. An hour had passed, and he'd stared at it, not hungry and not sure what he would do for the rest of the day.

He could show Brooke around some more, if that's what she wished. Anything she wanted, he wanted to give to her. It was his own needs that confused him. Keeping her happy was easy to devote himself to, for now.

Once she became a full-fledged member of the court, he had to go. Even if it tore at him, he knew the odds of their relationship ever being approved were dismal.

He'd once been smitten with the Duchess of Lugh Isle, and Catriona had disapproved. The Duchess was as equal to his station as possible, yet they'd been deemed an incompatible match. With those odds, he'd never be allowed to be with a human.

And there was no way he would stick around to see who they *would* approve of for Brooke.

Before he met Brooke, he had a plan. He had to stick to

that plan, even if it threatened to rip a hole in his chest. Sticking around wouldn't be good for either of them.

The front door creaked open and closed, and he hopped up to see how Brooke's tea went with the queen.

Instead of his curvy redheaded delight, he found Vevina skulking around the living room.

"What are you doing here?" he demanded. "Thought of another way to meddle in our lives?"

"Kerren..." She paused where she stood and turned sorrowful eyes at him.

Deep blue waves pulsed through her white hair. Regret. Sadness. He couldn't remember the last time she'd appeared this distraught. She was his family's servant by birth, but they'd always been more like friends.

It had been his decision to elevate her status. He made her his assistant and let her do mostly as she pleased. They did almost everything together, really. Up until her betrayal, he'd thought they were nearly family.

Now, he felt no pity for her.

"I asked you a question."

"I came to see you. I wanted to explain—"

"There's no excusing your actions, Vevina. What did I do to you that made you bitter enough to run off and spout your story? What did Brooke do to you?"

Vevina hung her head. "I came to seek your forgiveness, but I'd still appreciate it if you'd allow me to speak."

"Then speak," he said, waving a hand. "Please, tell me why you think you deserve my time."

She took a step toward him, then hesitated and shifted on her feet. "You can't leave, Kerren. Don't you see? You belong here. Your people love you."

"What does that have to do with anything?"

"Brooke fits in well, doesn't she? I knew the moment I

saw her. She would've been so happy if you would've brought her back home."

"Vevina..." he warned. "Make your point so you can leave."

"Why do you hate us all so much?" she demanded.

He pinched the bridge of his nose. "I don't hate Sidera Luminis. I'm just bored. I'm stifled. There's no future for me here."

"Because you say so, but for no real reason. You're barely even here!" she exclaimed. "You spend most of your time exploring the other planets. Why can't you just say what you mean? You're lonely."

"So what if I am?"

"Brooke is perfect," she said, worrying her hands on her dress. "Don't you see? This was supposed to make you happy —both of you happy. She wanted this. I have an entire profile for her. She wants someone just like you, and you need someone just like her."

"You're not making sense—we just met. And you spent what... half a day with her? You know nothing."

Certainly, he knew his feelings for Brooke, but there was no evidence she felt the same. It's not like she'd asked him to stay.

"I lied about Brooke," Vevina said carefully. "I didn't find her from an agency. I... made a dating profile for you with a paranormal matchmaking specialist."

The absurdity made him want to laugh, and he did. He walked to his couch and fell upon it. "That's ridiculous, even for you. This isn't one of your best games, Vevina. You can't play with Brooke's future and expect me to laugh it off."

"I'm not joking. This... Euphrasie has made so many happy endings come true, her reputation is known across the damn galaxy. And she matched Brooke with you."

"She's gorgeous. But chemistry isn't love, Vevina." He leaned forward and pulled a decanter of dark liquor towards him on the coffee table. Pouring a serving into a crystal glass, he sighed. "Brooke and I may have had a future had you not interfered. But now? Even if I wanted to pursue her, I'd be denied."

"Never. Brooke is your future."

Somehow, hearing Vevina make such a statement was like a punch to the gut. "You're right about one thing," he admitted. "I was lonely. I wanted a wife and a family. But you don't get to choose that for me, and some woman I've never met—matchmaker or no—doesn't get to choose that for me either."

"But… Don't you feel it?"

He took a sip of the amber liquid and closed his eyes as it burned and slid down his throat. Once the fire subsided, he looked at her. "Do you think that relationship would ever be approved? Don't you remember the last time I tried?"

"That selkie whore? Of course it wasn't approved. Every cock North of the Fade has petitioned to court Mira, Duchess of Lust Isle," Vevina shrieked. "No one will ever get approved for her. She has no class, paltry manners, and her territory will be dissolved within the next two centuries."

"We are equal—"

"You are so far above Mira she'd need a wisp to find the soles of your feet, Kerren. Besides, all of fae knows the love of selkies is the waters. You deserve more than to come second to *water*."

"And if Artur and Catriona don't agree? Brooke is having a hard enough time accepting this. If I tell her how I feel, only to have our relationship disapproved, what then?"

"Catriona is descended from a deity of love. She isn't inept. You keep assuming she'll say no just because it's you, and just because she kept you from making a mistake decades ago."

"Yet she and Artur approved my parents."

Vevina pursed her lips and her eyes trailed away. "That was different."

"How?" he asked.

He truly never understood his parents' relationship. His mother was sweet and free-spirited. His father was a drunken bully.

Vevina shifted on her feet. "You should ask your mother."

"I can't ask her. You know she hates speaking of him. She's happy now, and I won't dredge up old memories and make her upset." He turned to fully face Vevina. "But you know everything."

"Haven't you guessed by now?" she asked softly.

A knot tightened in his stomach. Years ago, he'd guessed. But this secret, like most of his memories of his childhood, was always locked away. "I was an accident."

She didn't deny his statement, only ran an idle hand along the sofa arm. Fae couples rarely conceived. They could be together for centuries and produce no children. Sexuality was open and casual relationships common. His mother had to have had the worst luck in the world.

There was no law that she had to marry, but it made sense that she thought it was for the best.

"Peter wasn't always a... tyrant. He used to be just... I don't know. Passionate? He thought he could settle down and be a dad. He wanted to try. I watched him try," Vevina insisted. "But it wasn't in his nature. He was selfish, and even the best intentions could become sour..."

"I don't need to hear. It's enough, just to know, finally," he murmured. "If my mother had raised me alone, I'd have been better off. A bastard duke is still a duke, and to the fae, any child is a blessing."

"Except that Bledwen has never been steady enough to rule. She is caring and sweet, but a focused woman, she is not," Vevina said hesitantly. "She had hoped that Peter could provide balance."

"And she was wrong." Kerren loved his mother dearly, but a mistake was a mistake.

"This doesn't have any bearing on your own relationships, Kerren. You aren't your father."

Unless Kerren had inherited his father's selfish nature. Unless good intentions and failed results ran in his blood.

He shook his head. "You shouldn't have tampered with fate, Vevina. Brooke may be better here—I don't know. I think she'd shine anywhere. But me? This world isn't for me."

"It is! You're just too stubborn to see past what you fear could happen. You don't want to put down your roots."

"You don't understand. My life here is empty." He swirled the glass in his hand and took another sip. "I can't serve the Barrows and watch my life pass by."

"You are the noblest man to rule the Barrows in a long while, and I should know since I served your bastard of a father," Vevina said firmly. "You think we don't need you, but we do. I'm speaking for all of your people. We want you to stay. We need your spirit to protect us."

"Protect you from what? The chill of winter?"

"You know that the province gains from the merits of the leadership, and just as equally, suffers from the flaws. Under you, we've seen growth and happiness. Safety." She came close and placed a hand on his shoulder, though he glared at her. "And that was with you barely trying. Imagine how we would fare with you at your best. Brooke is your future and ours. I wasn't trying to tamper with fate. I thought I was doing fate's bidding."

"Well, you're a fool," he muttered.

"If the end result is you coming to your senses and staying here, it's worth being a fool. If your life is empty, you fill it with something. Moving won't help you if you make the same choices."

"Yet you've set the course for Brooke to do just that—move in the hopes of something better," he scoffed. "You should leave before Brooke returns. She'll do better to adjust without having to see you."

Vevina squeezed his shoulder and stepped away. She seemed to want to say more, but after a quiet moment she turned and left.

Kerren lifted the crystal glass and rested its cool surface against his forehead. He didn't want to question fate or love or chemistry. He just wanted to see Brooke happy, even if that meant she lived a long life in Sidera Luminis without him.

Phones didn't work in Sidera Luminis, or at least most didn't. Technology, in general, tended to react to the magic atmosphere in strange ways. The exception was a certain line of computers made specifically for Sidera Luminis, and even then, they had limited capabilities—but they could be used for short voice calls.

Luckily, Vevina had one in her office in the home. She was always on top of all things new and couldn't live without her handheld organizer.

Kerren pressed the power button on the computer and momentarily regretted sending her away before getting to the bottom of her matchmaking scheme. He needed to speak to the woman who had placed Brooke into his employ.

The computer loaded quickly and Kerren scanned the desktop for any clues. A notification for a new email from

Euphrasie popped up in the corner and he clicked it, immediately recalling the familiar name.

The email was checking in to see how things were moving along since Brooke wasn't answering her phone. The message had a number at the bottom, which he clicked and waited on while the computer dialed out.

"Hello?" a mature woman's voice answered.

"Hello. Is this Celestial Soul Mates, Inc?" he asked.

"In a way. You've reached Euphrasie and I'm one of the many representatives. I assume if you have this number we're working together? Who do I have the pleasure of speaking to today?"

"Kerren Aodhán."

"Oh, the fae duke, yes. Tell me, how is everything with Brooke?"

He slouched in his chair and stared at the computer screen. "Ah… she's fine. But I've got some unfortunate news for you, about the entire situation."

"Oh dear… go on."

"I never created a dating profile with your agency. My assistant did."

"Oh? Well you'd be surprised at how often that happens. Luckily at Celestial Soul Mates we have ways of verifying our clientele by other means."

"But how—"

"It's quite rare that someone submits a profile quite as deeply honest as yours."

"Yes, well. That's problem one, since I didn't submit anything. Problem two is that it doesn't seem like Brooke was looking for a match either."

"Did she say that?"

"No, not exactly. But she came as a guide—"

"Yes, yes. Brooke is stubborn, but unless your assistant's details about you were misleading, she's your match. I just assumed that you would tell her that you wanted more than a tour guide, and the rest would handle itself."

Kerren cleared his throat, recalling how quickly he and Brooke had gone from tour to bedroom. "Well, there was certainly chemistry… but if neither of us was looking, haven't we done this wrong?"

Euphrasie's laugh rang as clear as a bell. "Wonderful. You know, I expect this sort of nonsense from wolves and bears and such, but I thought a duke of the fae would see clearer."

"Pardon?"

The rustling of paper being moved and crinkled came across the line, then Euphrasie asked, "Do you ever travel?"

"Yes. Quite often, actually."

"Would you consider yourself to be charming and intellectual, yet capable of being at home at either a fancy dinner party or relaxing with a beer?" she continued as if reading from something.

Kerren tilted his head side to side in consideration. "Sidera Luminis doesn't have Earth-style beer, but I suppose yes."

"And are you so desperately lonely that you'd leave your life behind, come to a city you've never heard of on a planet you've never been to, and hire a dating agency to find your true love?"

"But I didn't—"

"Are we talking, or not, dear?" she asked seriously.

He ran a hand through his hair. "I suppose, even though I did not hire you, that is disturbingly accurate."

"If you didn't want to hire me, you wouldn't have contacted me to tell me about this so-called mix-up. Be honest. You wanted to make sure Brooke was your match, not correct me for sending you someone you didn't want," she chided.

"Are all Americans so blunt?" he muttered not meaning for her to hear.

"Delightfully so," she replied. "I can't force you to do anything, clearly. But even though I detest being tricked, the match was still a match. If it helps, think of my suggestion as being written in the stars. I am very good at what I do."

"I see."

"I don't know what you two are up to, but please tell Brooke she can call me anytime."

"Of course. Thank you, I suppose."

"Mmhmm. You be good."

The line went quiet and the call clicked off. Euphrasie's certainty shook him, except for one thing. Maybe desperation wasn't the best foundation to form a relationship on.

CHAPTER 11

BROOKE

The sun was setting by the time Brooke made her way back to Kerren's manor. It hadn't been her intention to be away all day, but after leaving the Queen's garden she'd gone for a walk to think about what little they'd discussed.

She searched through the quiet house looking for Kerren, eventually finding him in the backyard. Strange lights hovered in the air around him, and once she got closer she realized they were small fae.

Her hands covered her mouth to catch her gasp, in case they'd be scared away. Still, Kerren turned and noticed her.

"There you are." He stood and walked to meet her. "I was worried until I was told you weren't alone."

"Right," she said, still staring at the glowing fae. "One of the guards followed me around to keep me from getting too lost. He wouldn't share his name. Awkward, really, but that doesn't matter. Fairies?"

He glanced to where she stared. "Pixies. Precocious demi-fae, and easy to invite over. When they have sweets, they become quite celebratory."

"They're tiny... do they talk?"

He nodded and placed a hand on her back, guiding her forward. "They do, but perhaps not tonight. When I sprinkled the honey crystals, I wasn't considering the frost globes on the other side of the garden."

"What are those?"

"Fae fruit that tends to over-ripen and ferment on the vine."

"They're drunk?" she asked with a half-laugh.

"Drunk and hyper. Fun to watch right now while they're dancing, but soon enough my yard is going to be hosting a demifae orgy." He sighed and shook his head. "Sorry. It seemed like a promising idea this morning."

Brooke chuckled softly, watching the pixies dance as if the night breeze was a melody. "You brought them here to see me?"

"I thought you would enjoy their company. And I'm certain if they weren't in their current state they'd want to meet you."

"I appreciate it."

They stood and observed the tiny fae in quiet for a few moments, but as Kerren had predicted, dancing soon turned to groping.

"Ready for dinner?" Kerren asked.

The day had felt long already, and though normally stress made her eat, she'd felt almost too anxious to be hungry. Almost.

"I'm curious to see what sort of dinner you have here." As the words left her mouth, her stomach growled. "Okay, I guess I'm hungrier than I thought. It seems like I haven't eaten enough since I got here."

"Don't worry. It's a temporary side-effect of traveling through the portal. Something about the time change, I think." The kitchen lit as he stepped in and opened the cupboard.

Though most of Sidera Luminis seemed less than modern, it still surprised Brooke to see how magic could replace technology in a nearly seamless manner. Until now, she hadn't realized that there was no light switch in this room—or any of the rooms.

Instead, candles lined the walls and sat on tables, ready to flicker on at the appearance of people. They gave more light than traditional candles and burned a soft white rather than dim yellow.

Much like the self-heating and pampering tub, she wondered if this magic was standard or a luxury.

"Does everyone live like this?" she asked.

"How do you mean?" He didn't look up from his task of slicing a large loaf of bread and arranging the pieces on a plate.

"The candles and the overall… ease of magic." She sat on a stool and watched him.

He opened a small jar containing what appeared to be an orange spread and placed it on the plate before pushing it towards her. "Something to snack on while I cook," he explained, then leaned on the counter with furrowed brows. "Yes and no. There is a cost for magic. Not financial but… something intangible. Being fae, it simply happens and makes sense to me. It's different for all the different fae. Brownies, for example, always have spotless homes that feel comfortable."

"That sounds nice," Brooke said and scooped a piece of bread through the spread.

"It truly is. You could sit in a Brownie's living room and it will simply feel like home and have all the comforts of a home. They don't need to buy food. It's always around. They don't need blankets because the temperature is always right, but any blankets they offer you will be the softest you've ever held."

"Wow." She tried to imagine such a thing. "I'd like to experience that someday."

"I'm sure you will. The Barrows has a large Brownie population, and they love guests. Just be sure to bring them gifts. Company should always bring gifts to Brownies unless the visit wasn't intended. Which happens—they are likely to welcome you in straight off the streets," he said with a laugh.

He'd pulled some vegetables from below the counter and now chopped them. The fae versions of onions, carrots, and cabbage, from what she could guess. She took a bite of her bread and was pleasantly surprised. The dip tasted sweet yet cheesy.

"Oh my goodness," she marveled.

"I thought you'd like that. This spread's recipe has been in my family since the beginning of time—or so they say."

"You made it?"

"I did. I enjoy cooking." He minced a small brown root and set the knife down. "It's even more enjoyable when I'm with someone who appreciates it."

"I certainly appreciate food, and you make a sexy chef," she agreed. "But what about humans with no magic?"

Tearing the leaves of a strange teal plant, he shrugged. "I'm actually not sure. But as nobility, you'll have servants, and their magic will infuse to wherever you live. Like an impression."

"I don't want servants," she said with a slight frown. "I can take care of myself."

"Some fae live to serve, Brooke. It's not a position without perks and respect." He tossed everything into a pot and sprinkled various seasonings into it. "But if you'd like, simply promote someone to be your assistant, as I did. Vevina was bound to my family through a blood-debt incurred long before I was born, but I hated the idea of a life-long servant."

"Blood-debt?" Brooke asked. "So she's your servant forever?"

"Assistant. And yes, for her life. Before you ask, I can't revoke it—that would be disrespectful to her entire lineage."

"The fae are strange."

He grinned. "To you. But Vevina's magic is what soothed you in the tub, for example. Though I suspect she left a quite intentional imprint there. She lives for bubble baths."

A flicker of sadness crossed his expression, and unless she was mistaken, the lights momentarily dimmed. Vevina had served him—been by his side—most of his life. It was hard to imagine how he felt, but she knew there was little she could do to help. What was between them could only be solved by them.

"What sort of fae is Vevina?"

"She's part naiad, part other things... but her story isn't mine to tell."

Brooke leaned forward, head tilting in curiosity. "You've told me about others, though."

"I have. Vevina though... aside from the fact that she tells it better, if I tell you what she is you'll have endless questions."

"Ah."

"What did the Queen say?" he asked.

"Not much, actually. But what she did say made me realize that my protests about moving to Sidera Luminis are... silly."

"I wouldn't call wanting to live your own life silly," he disagreed.

He turned and filled the pot with water, then set it over the fire.

"I left my phone in your hotel room," she said, stirring the bread through the creamy spread. "And I haven't missed it. I woke up this morning and something was missing… the dread of having to sit at a desk for ten hours while being unappreciated and underpaid. I have wanted to make a million changes to my life, and I have the opportunity now. I'm over how I got here, and I'm eager to take advantage of it."

He smiled and stirred the pot with a long-handled wooden spoon. "You make Sidera Luminis seem… fresh. I suppose growing up here, it doesn't have the same sparkle to me."

"The grass is always greener on the other side," Brooke commented.

"What's that?"

"A saying. The grass is always greener… It's easy to look at someone else's life or something you don't have, and it will seem better than your life or what you have."

He appeared thoughtful and set the spoon down on the counter before moving to the island where she sat. He tore off a small piece of bread and ate it, watching her intently.

"Is something wrong?" she asked, feeling self-conscious.

"I'm relieved that you will be fine here. I couldn't have left knowing you were going to be miserable for eternity."

Her heart tumbled. For a while, she'd forgotten their impending separation. "You're eager to explore Earth some more? You'll need a new guide."

He nodded. His eyes had lost their sparkle, and he seemed lost in thought.

"I wish you'd stay," she said softly.

"I'm not sure if it would be wise for me to. It could be like you say, that I'm imagining that things would be better somewhere else simply because I'm not there. Or it could be like your situation, where I need to go where I have the opportunity to create a better life."

She knew what he meant, though the thought of being apart filled her with a hollow sensation. Her feelings for Kerren were clear in her heart, and she suspected he knew and felt the same way.

But is that enough for him to change his dreams? If I tell him what I want and ask him to stay, is it smart or is it selfish?

"Dinner's ready," he announced.

BROOKE ROLLED over and stared at the gauzy curtains hiding the moon and stars. The bed in Kerren's guest room was easily as large and comfortable as his own bed, and he'd revealed that it was once his room growing up. Still, it felt lonely here. The house was massive but empty.

She couldn't imagine how he stood it, and it gave her insight as to why he'd leave. What was the point of the magic lights and pixies and fancy furniture without people? Surely Kerren had friends? More family?

It didn't make sense. He was a duke. She just assumed he'd be surrounded by others at all times. He'd mentioned servants, but she'd never seen a soul around the manor.

The sound of gentle footsteps down the hall made her sit up and look at the door. It creaked open and Kerren entered slowly.

"Ah. You aren't asleep," he commented.

"And if I was?"

He didn't say anything but sat on the edge of the bed. "I don't know, really. Maybe I just wanted to be creepy and watch you sleep."

"Your honesty is so refreshing," she joked.

"I'll go," he said.

"No." She pulled the covers back and patted the bed beside her. "Lay with me? I'm having trouble falling asleep."

The bed dipped as he climbed on and scooted beside her. His body curled against hers familiarly, as if this was typical. They fit together well.

"I know why I can't sleep, but what about you? I thought you were at peace with everything," he whispered.

"Just thoughts. I tend to over-think things. My brain is awake and analyzing too much. It's not unusual."

He kissed her shoulder and sighed against her neck, his breath warm and tickling her skin.

"You live alone in this huge mansion," she said carefully.

"I do. It's been in the family forever, I'm told. But once, servants lived here, and families had many generations."

"Where is your family? Don't you have cousins? Aunts? Uncles?" she asked.

"Cousins all over, yes. One aunt. No uncles. The fae don't usually have more than one or two children."

"Why not?"

"We simply don't. We don't procreate as easily as humans, just as humans don't procreate as easily as rabbits. It's related to life expectancy, I suppose."

"The fae live long..." Her eyes widened. "Oh my... fuck."

"Something wrong?"

"The Queen said the King was two hundred. I meant to ask about it but something else came up and I just forgot... how long do you live?"

He grew quiet, and she turned over to face him. His eyes were open and staring at her, but he seemed deep in thought.

"Kerren?"

"We live as long as we live. Very few of the fae are the type to suffer from old age, though it does happen. Other-wise... forever."

"And the humans?"

"The same. That's part of why humans have to be claimed. Except for rare exceptions—you, for example—the humans share their extended lives with whoever claimed them. Individuals or even entire bloodlines. Depends on how they choose to have it done," he explained. "I feel like a fool. I didn't say anything. I didn't even think of it."

"But you're leaving Sidera Luminis."

"Yes. And if I'm away long enough, I lose that immortality. I'd age."

"And you're okay with that?" She searched his face.

"If it meant happiness, yes. I've lived... I'm not two hundred, but..." He swept his hand over her cheek. "You're going to ask, so for the record, I'm only a little over twice your human age."

She took a deep breath and rolled over to lay on her back and stare at the ceiling. The news was shocking, and she couldn't begin to unravel how this fit in with the other adaptations.

She'd thought of living forever before. Not seriously, but rationally. The sort of theorizing one did with friends when drinking beers and watching a vampire movie.

What will I do with forever?

"But wouldn't everyone get bored eventually? Sick of each other?"

"That's what the Fade is for. It's where the fae can go to rest. It can be temporary or permanent. Like a long nap." He propped himself up on one elbow and watched her. "Are you okay? I can't imagine the sort of shock..."

A tear rolled down her cheek, though she didn't know why. Shock. Fear. Whatever emotion she had, she couldn't identify it. Maybe it was hope.

"I'm fine," she said shakily. "But hold me?"

He pulled her to lay across his chest, brushing his fingers through her wild hair. He pressed his lips to the top of her head and said, "I wish I knew what to say to make it better."

Tell me you love me and that you'll stay. Aloud all she could offer was, "Just another thing to add to my to-be-pondered list."

She stroked his muscled chest and toyed with the tiny patch of hair that tickled her cheek. For a hound, he was actually quite smooth in this form. She pressed herself closer to him and lifted her head to kiss his cheek.

Flames flickered to life in his eyes, faint but noticeable. She kissed his mouth and shuddered as his arms wrapped tight around her. She didn't want more tonight, but she needed this for now.

Drawing back, she trapped his lower lip between her teeth and simply stared at him, losing herself in the glowing green fire. She let go and smiled.

Returning to the comfortable spot under his arm and pressed against his body, she released a deep breath. Forever would be a long time to be without Kerren.

CHAPTER 12

KERREN

*K*erren woke to the sound of a gasp. He rubbed his eyes and ran a hand through his hair, then sat up. He didn't need to ask what surprised her because now he saw for himself. Leaning against one of the bedposts and staring at them both was Lorelei.

She twirled a lock of white-blonde hair around her fingertip and pursed her lips as if holding back a laugh.

"To what do we owe this pleasure?" he asked dryly.

As long as he was back on Sidera Luminis he had to be polite to the Queen's personal messenger, even if he wanted nothing more than to send Lorelei packing. Her pale gold eyes zeroed in on him.

"Royal summons," she announced mysteriously.

"Again?" Brooke asked. "Wait. Now am I in trouble?"

Lorelei shook her head. "No trouble, just summoned. And this time, I come for His Grace, though you are welcome to attend as a soon-to-be member of the court. I was told you may arrive at your leisure, but I will add personally that sooner would be preferred."

"Let me guess. Within the hour, you'd say?" Kerren asked.

"The King and Queen seemed a bit... anxious," Lorelei said carefully. "But you didn't hear that from me," she added with a wink.

"And I suppose you can't say what this is regarding," he guessed.

She shook her head. "I do apologize. It's quite rare that I'm sent out with such little information. First, Brooke's questioning, now this. You know I'm usually much more in the loop."

Lorelei certainly wasn't lying. Kerren had been summoned before, but there was usually an apparent reason. Summons weren't meant to be secretive, after all.

Usually, it was to face a punishment for a discovered crime, or on more pleasant circumstances, to award something. Occasionally, Lorelei was used in lieu of a paper invitation to formal gatherings—which was the highest form of flattery.

Being dropped in on out of the blue not once, but twice, was severely trying on Kerren's patience, and he could only guess how Brooke felt to awaken to a stranger watching her yet again.

"We'll be there as soon as we've eaten," he said. He did his best to keep his annoyance out of his voice. Glancing to Brooke, who sat silently beside him, he clarified, "I assume you'd like to accompany me? See the proceedings from a guest seat rather than a spotlight?"

"I wouldn't miss it. I'm curious to see what you've done this time around," she said with a grin.

He turned to Lorelei. "There you go. We'll be there."

"Wonderful." She took a step back and dissolved into a cloud of gold and pink glitter.

Kerren groaned and fell back, head hitting the pillow with a gentle thump. "I detest when she does that. And the staff won't be by to clean it since technically I no longer live here."

"What?"

"The floor."

The bed shook gently as Brooke crawled her way to the edge.

"Oh my God, she left literal glitter. I thought that was just a magic thing, like the flame from when you changed," Brooke squealed. "Wow. That's actually super cool."

He laughed and placed a hand to his brow. Of course, she'd be amused by it.

"Your reaction is probably why she did it. Lorelei is a sprite. She revels in all things… flashy. She doesn't have to toss confetti or smoke or in this case, glitter, but she can and will if it'll make a point." He sat back up and crawled behind Brooke, wrapping his arms around her and looking over her shoulder at his sparkling carpet. "I could burn things with my fire but generally I see no purpose. Though, I'm not one for the dramatic."

"I guess we should get dressed and see what's going on?"

He nuzzled her neck and wondered if there was a chance of subtly hinting at his current morning stiffness. "I'm not really in a hurry…"

"Hmm, but I'm starving. I'll help you cook this time?"

The slight whine to her voice made him abandon hope of a pre-breakfast quickie. Then he was struck with the more obvious issue. He slid from the bed and stepped around the contaminated floor. "Sounds fair. Guess I'll scamper off and let you get dressed."

"Yup. I'll be down in a few," she promised.

He headed out and pulled the door shut behind him. Leaning back against the wood, he made a decision. After the summon, he'd ask Catriona for permission to have a relationship with Brooke. The sex and flirting weren't enough. He needed more and was tired of giving in to unnecessary insecurities.

Every fiber of his being knew that Brooke was the one. They were in sync and at ease. He found himself touching her as if to remind himself she was real. Now he just had to make sure that she always would be.

KERREN STOOD in the center of the royal emblem on the tile floor of the throne room, watching King Artur and Queen Catriona whisper to each other. To his left, Brooke sat surrounded by the fae who were now her peers. They seemed to be getting along well, and it didn't escape his notice that some of the fae capable of glamour—changing their appearance at will—had already stolen her bright ruby hair color.

He couldn't help the smile that crested his lips at seeing her chatting away, though her eyes constantly returned to him.

"Kerren Aodhán, Duke and protector of the esteemed Weylan Barrows, you are called to the court, so we may have witnesses over this proceeding," King Artur finally announced.

His eyes regarded Kerren with more attention than he'd ever warranted before from the King. Kerren kept his rigid posture and neutral expression. He could have asked what was going on, but he'd know soon enough. For now, silence was fine with him.

Artur settled back in his chair and rubbed his temple with one hand while the other squeezed around Catriona's finger-tips. Catriona stared at Kerren with a strange expression, one he didn't recognize but that put him on guard.

Possibilities of what he could have done wrong flashed through his mind, but nothing stuck.

"Many years ago, my dear Catriona and I kept a secret. And enough time has passed that perhaps the few others that knew of it have forgotten it," Artur said in a clear voice. "That secret was a pregnancy."

The hum of whispers crept over the room until Artur held up a hand and commanded silence.

"It was a secret because of one thing that all have known: Catriona and I have not been able to produce an heir," he continued. He looked at his wife, who turned her head away, eyes clenched tight. "The child was carried to term but died immediately before labor. We kept our secret, and our child was buried that night."

He stopped for a moment and kissed his wife's hand. Kerren wanted to ask what this story had to do with his summoning, but the King's confession was heartbreaking. As rare as children were, to lose one as he had was devastating. Emotions welled through the room, and with enough fae experiencing it, the effect became tangible, like a weight on his shoulders.

Catriona leaned forward now. "Our midwife handled the burial. I was too stricken with grief, and weak besides. She left Sidera Luminis a few days later, which we assumed was due to her own pain through the ordeal. With everything else, we didn't question it. But recently we called upon her."

The side doors to the room opened and a guard escorted a frail young woman into the room. At the same time, another guard approached Kerren. He held a robe over his arm and bowed slightly as he came close.

"Kerren. Few know your spirit form, and I would not normally expose a fellow shifter, but I would ask you to please reveal yourself."

Brooke's gasp was distinguishable from the low chatter of the rest of the room. Kerren kept his eyes forward, studying Catriona and Artur for any indication of reason. After a moment, he unbuttoned his shirt and pushed down his pants. Nudity wasn't scandalous among the fae, but for nobility there were standards.

Still, he wasn't ashamed of his body, and a royal command wasn't one to be ignored. He kicked his boots off and gave Brooke a cheeky smile. If nothing else, he didn't want her to be worried.

Looking back to the King and Queen, with his hands modestly hiding his package, he concentrated on summoning his spirit forward. It wasn't something that usually required thought, but the surrounding audience made it skittish. His skin tingled and warmed. Within a flash of green fae fire, he changed.

Now a cu sidhe, he took a step forward and circled before sitting. He used his form to hunt occasionally or to enjoy the wilds, but for the most part, he'd kept it secret. The loud din that now rose was exactly why.

Enough fae still lived that had seen his cu sidhe brethren through the war. They were scouts and heroes. The sight of the large green hound-beast brought tears to many eyes, and this group was no exception. His form was a symbol of triumph but also burden and loss.

The Queen was stricken as well, he noticed. As her tears fell he wondered why she would request to see what would only distress her. The King stood and snapped his fingers.

"Arrest Lady Sibeal," he announced.

The confusion and chatter rose, and Kerren shifted back to his upright state, quickly snatching the robe from the guard and donning it. He looked back and saw Sibeal held by two guards, a wild look in her eyes.

"I didn't want to believe such treachery," Artur roared. "I didn't want to hear that my sister, my flesh and blood, ordered our midwife to dispose of our son so that her own son could take the throne."

"Mother!"

Kerren spun and saw Basil, Sibeal's son step forward.

"Is this true?" he demanded.

"I wanted the best for you! We've too long been under the reign of Brea's blood," Sibeal sobbed.

"But I didn't dispose of him," a soft voice said. Somehow it carried through the noise, and Kerren realized it was the soothing sound of a siren. The frail woman looked up and spoke again, "After the baby was born, he did not cry. It was easy to say he was stillborn. But I could not kill him, no matter what threats hung over my head and the heads of my family."

"Traitor!" Sibeal screamed. Madness filled her eyes, and the guards held her still. Dark bands of iron were clamped around her wrists to tamp down her magic temporarily. "One task for the sake of the Pure! Was it so much?"

The midwife ignored her, looking to Kerren. "That same night, Lady Bledwen did in fact miscarry. I brought the child to her before any knew the wiser. But even though I lied and told Lady Sibeal I'd followed her wishes, to please spare my family, she banished me off-world. She said if I returned she would haunt us all."

"But..." Kerren frowned as the pieces came together. He looked to Catriona and finally recognized the emotion tearing her apart.

"Son," she called softly. "How did I never see? You have my eyes."

A hush fell over the room as she and Artur stood and walked down the steps from their thrones to meet Kerren. He didn't understand, or rather, a large part of him denied this revelation.

"You have our brand," Artur remarked. "Our royal marking, the sign of blessing from the aspects. And if you were a more boastful man, we would have seen it sooner."

"The cu sidhe is a proud spirit, but not a braggart," Kerren said dumbfounded.

"We had kept the royal marking's specifics a secret, but there is no reason to hide it any longer," Artur replied.

Catriona fell against Kerren, hugging him tight while weeping openly. "My son. The aspects have answered my pleas."

Kerren stood still though his arms reached around his Queen—no, his mother. And though Bledwen had raised him with love, he still had room to welcome this new discovery. The more he looked at her, the more he saw the familiarity in Catriona's eyes.

Wild and mixed genetics meant the fae didn't always resemble their parents, so he'd never wondered about not looking like Bledwen and Peter.

Yet, standing between Artur and Catriona he saw the slight markings. Artur's hair, though dark like night, had hints of green buried in the depths, and he shared Kerren's same sharp nose. Catriona's high cheekbones made him feel like he looked into a mirror.

Artur encased both Kerren and Catriona into a severe embrace as Kerren struggled to find words to express his state. He turned his head, hoping to spy Brooke and read her face and take comfort in her presence. At the mere thought of her, the responsibilities and expectations of royalty came tumbling forward, stirring new fear in Kerren's stomach.

If as a duke I was rejected to a duchess, could I then as a prince be bound to a human?

He leaned close to Catriona, squeezing his eyes shut as he spilled forth what he hoped would be an easily accepted request. The words came whispered but full of emotion.

"I wish to marry the human, Brooke."

CHAPTER 13

BROOKE

*B*rooke sat in a state of shock, feeling as if the world had frozen for her even if it continued to move for everyone else. The fae around her were carrying on wildly, but she was speechless. She stared at Kerren and wondered how he felt, to discover after so many years that his life wasn't the one intended for him.

"Brooke?" a familiar voice called.

She turned and saw Vevina watching her. A hint of anger still lingered in her heart towards Vevina, even if she had accepted a life on Sidera Luminis.

"Yes?"

"The Queen sent me… well, Kerren wanted to be sure you made it home. It seems they've got quite a bit to discuss, of course," Vevina said with a careful smile.

Brooke took in Vevina's appearance. It had been shocking to see her fae form at first, but the more she looked, the more fitting it seemed. Without needing to ask, she'd come to realize that Vevina's hair somehow reflected her mood, even if Brooke didn't understand what each color meant.

But if she had to guess by the stark white roots and peach tips, Vevina was just as surprised as she was.

"I haven't really forgiven you," Brooke admitted. "I feel like I should put that out there."

Vevina's smile fell and she nodded. "Kerren hasn't either. Still, I am bound by duty and harbor nothing but good will towards you. I believe Sidera Luminis was always meant to be your home."

The honesty in Vevina's voice was clear. Brooke didn't want to hold a grudge, but that didn't mean she could ignore what happened. "Maybe I was going to end up here another way, but we'll never know now."

Vevina glanced over her shoulder and Brooke followed her gaze. Kerren and the King and Queen were leaving, walking towards the doors behind the raised platform their thrones sat on.

"I guess I may as well head home," Brooke said. "I mean… Kerren's home."

She stood and followed Vevina through the crowd. Once they left the boisterous assembly, she walked beside the small fae.

"Kerren doesn't look much like them," Brooke remarked.

"I can see it in small ways. But that's not strange. I look nothing like my parents. I look exactly like my grandmother though, and that's where I got my magic," Vevina explained.

Brooke tried to understand what she meant. "You inherit the magic and the appearance?"

"Something like that. There are physical traits that are related to abilities. A succubus will always be gorgeous. A selkie will always have brown hair and brown eyes. And now that I know that Kerren's father is Artur, that… raises interesting questions."

"How so?"

"Kerren looks like the forest, and Artur is half forest

deity. I bet Kerren has latent magic that hasn't come forward yet," Vevina explained. She walked with her head down and hands in her pockets. "Kerren's father—or rather, the one he grew up with—was a shifter too. Not cu sidhe, but shifters don't always inherit the same form, save for selkies. Now that he knows he has a forest spirit, new magic will come."

"That's crazy. I can't imagine how he went this long… I mean, no one suspected a thing," Brooke mused.

"We always thought his appearance came from Bledwen's side—since she has plant related lineage. Yet Kerren is far from having a green thumb, no matter how often he tries."

"He has a lovely garden," Brooke pointed out.

"Yes. Thanks to a lovely dryad who lives on the grounds," Vevina said with a snort. "Everything started to die when Bledwen moved out, so Kara moved in."

"I haven't seen anyone else around. In fact, it seems like the manor is quite lonely."

"Kara lives in her tree. When I said moved in, I didn't mean in the usual way. Dryads are attached to a single tree. She came to be when a seed took root on the land, but it was done on purpose. Kara's mother made a deal with the breeze to have her blown over…" Vevina's voice trailed off and she glanced at Brooke. "It's a whole… thing. Sorry. I'm usually better at explaining things."

"No, thank you. It's amazing. I love hearing about everything," Brooke said with a smile.

Vevina seemed to brighten slightly, and Brooke took pity.

"May I ask what about you? What was your grandmother?"

Vevina glanced up at the sky. "A sprite."

"Oh. Like Lorelei?"

Vevina grinned. "Yes. Though we have different distinctions. My grandmother could trace her lineage back to the times when sprites changed the colors of the leaves, and further back still, to the aspects."

"Naiad and sprite… Kerren made it seem like there was more," Brooke commented.

"Oh, there's more. My parents were both shifters, obviously I didn't inherit that. Tiny bit of disappointment, honestly. My mother can turn into a fox and that seems fascinating." She let out a tiny sigh of disappointment. "But my grandfather was human," Vevina revealed. "And the reason I am indebted to the blood of Weylan Barrows."

Brooke paused. "Am I prying to want to know?"

Vevina shrugged. "It would be strange if you didn't want to know. You will be joining the Barrows for your ceremony, and I am part of the history."

They continued walking and Brooke peered over. Vevina seemed to be gathering her thoughts. After a few moments, she spoke up.

"I don't know how much Kerren explained of our past. I know he took you to the center, where they display the heroes."

"Oh, of the wars?"

"Yes. We are strange in that we keep them there, but rarely do we discuss the wars between the courts. Wars against others are easier to speak of than the wars we fought amongst ourselves," Vevina mused aloud.

Brooke nodded. Kerren had briefly touched on the way Sidera Luminis was divided. The Pure court reigned here, but far away there was another fae colony—the Virtuous court. And though Kerren saw both as doing what they believed was best, the history of wars spoke volumes.

"He mentioned the two courts."

"In our history we have fought three wars with the Virtuous. Over land, love, and life, in that order. You'll learn it all in time but understand that when it got to the point where each side believed the other was jeopardizing the lives of all, in fact, endangering the very existence of Sidera Luminis, that's what made it the cruelest of wars."

Brooke frowned as she listened, trying to imagine the fae she'd seen so far engaged in battle.

"Many feared extinction. That what the other side was doing would cause the aspects to unmake us all. The actions this caused during the war… well, they'd never gotten along perhaps, but it had never been hate-fueled before. And in that atmosphere, my grandfather made a decision."

"But he was only human," Brooke interjected.

"Yes. And perhaps that's why he did what he did. He had a child on the way and feared for everything," Vevina said with a sigh. "I'll spare the details. But trust me, just because you are human does not mean you are powerless. What he did destroyed an entire village. The deaths that followed…" her voice trailed off, and her hair had lost all color.

"My family was of the Virtuous court, so even if my grandfather acted alone, my grandmother, Helene, was expected to pay. The hunters came for my her, but before the cu sidhe could bay three times, Rhoan stepped in. Rhoan was the duke and protector of the Barrows back then, and even if it were war, even with all the death he'd seen, he refused to allow his men to mark a pregnant woman."

"I'm confused. Mark?"

Vevina nodded solemnly. "Cu sidhe can mark a soul for death, and to do so ensures eternal torment, to never find peace in the afterworld. But even though Rhoan had stopped those with him, Helene could never truly escape. Hounds have a pack mind. She would have been found eventually. Very few can hide from the cu sidhe."

"So she made a deal?" Brooke guessed.

"Yes. Pledged her allegiance to the Pure and offered her

blood as debt. As long as the line lives, it serves the Barrows. But before you get upset, it is not a burden."

"But you live forever, and your child will live forever…"

"The debt is renewed with each generation. I chose to keep up the tradition. The meaning is clear, isn't it? I am still grateful, and I don't feel in my heart that my family has paid the debt. And if I have a child, they will decide for themselves. But fae take honor seriously. Closing a blood-debt too soon is disrespectful to both sides."

Brooke watched the ground as they walked. She hadn't imagined that something this dark had lurked beneath Vevina and Kerren's past.

"He doesn't change, for your sake," Brooke said finally. "Because of your history with the cu sidhe."

"Yes," Vevina admitted. "I know I have nothing to fear, but yes."

Brooke had not doubted Kerren's depth of character, but this certainly said it all. To suppress his spirit form to avoid attention was one thing. To keep it hidden to keep his best friend at ease meant much more.

"What will you do if Kerren leaves?" she asked.

"He can't leave now. He's the prince."

"Oh. That's right." Brooke hadn't thought about it that deeply.

We have a chance now, though. We could try a relationship, why not?

Before she knew it, they'd arrived back at Kerren's home. Brooke looked down the long path to the front door, wondering if Kerren would move into the palace or continue living alone.

"I don't know when Kerren will return, but I've alerted the staff to return for now and maintain things. They'll cook and clean… but I don't think he'll be gone long. They can't expect to catch up in a single day," Vevina said.

"Thanks." Brooke wanted to invite Vevina inside, but she'd vanished before there was a chance. Unlike Lorelei, there was no burst of glitter, no show.

Brooke skipped entering the home and instead walked around to the back garden. She had a lot to talk to Kerren about, but he was going through enough right now. At least now they had time.

IT WAS LATE when Brooke heard Kerren return home. The day had gone by with no word from him, and though she understood why, she'd missed him. At one point someone had stopped by to measure her and plan her gown for her initiation ceremony the next day, and even that felt less exciting without Kerren around.

She was upstairs and looking out the window, listening to his footsteps through the house when a gentle knock sounded on her door. She turned, trying to hide her excitement.

"Come in," she called.

He entered with a strange expression on his face as if he was still in shock so many hours later. She couldn't blame him. He stood beside her and looked out the window the way she'd been doing just moments before. Below, the pixies were back, partying and indulging on ripe fruit.

Kerren had unintentionally birthed quite the rave atmosphere.

"Looks like I'll be staying," he commented. "Though I have to say, I'm not upset about that anymore."

"Yeah?"

"I'm not sure it's really sunk in. Even after spending the day with them, talking, making sense of everything—or at least, trying to—only a part of me seems to comprehend a thing," he said. His brows were raised, and he still looked outside. "It's too much, almost."

"I can't imagine."

"But change can be good, and I guess I needed it. A jolt. Something to put me back on track. And since I'm staying for good, I need to handle this first."

He turned to her and took her hands. She smiled at his warm touch and gazed into his eyes.

"I've asked permission to form a relationship with you, Brooke."

Her head tilted to the side, but she didn't say anything yet. She had thought they already had a relationship, albeit temporary. They hadn't labeled it, but she felt they had an unspoken agreement. *The way we behaved spoke volumes, didn't it?*

"I wasn't sure if I'd be granted the chance, but it's all fallen into place. I'm not leaving Sidera Luminis. And if I'm staying, I can't imagine not doing everything in my power to be with you," he said, squeezing her hands.

"Wow," she breathed. Her heart fell with his words—*if I'm staying.* As if she were a consolation prize. "I don't even know what to say."

"I know it's sudden, but I want to be with you forever," he continued.

She sucked in a deep breath and exhaled slowly. "Oh. Do you mean…"

"Yes. I want you to be my wi—"

"No."

He drew back, though he still held her hands. "Brooke?"

She yanked her hands free and took a few steps away. "I don't even know where to start."

"I'm confused. I thought we had something," he said flustered.

"We did have something. But it was between us, not us and your mother. If you wanted to be with me, why didn't you tell me first?"

"I told you, nobility has to have permission."

"But that doesn't mean you just ask before consulting me. Wouldn't it have made more sense for us to make that decision ourselves, then… I don't know… petitioned together? A united force?"

"I didn't think…"

"And do you think it's romantic that all of this is happening only because you no longer have the choice to leave? Just last night you were still ready to walk away from me. Now you want to marry me. Coincidence?"

"No, I'd decided—"

"Stop!" She wiped away tears that fell out of her frustration. "The one thing I can't stand for is being a fallback. A consolation wife. I love you, and I thought that somehow, we'd find a way because I couldn't stand the thought of living here without you. But if you can only be with me because you have no choice—I don't want you."

He stepped forward, hands held out as if he meant to hold her, but she walked away.

"That's not what I meant. It's not because of that, it's because of us. We're meant to be together," he offered.

She held the post of the bed and stared at him. "I don't believe in settling, Kerren. And right now, it sure feels like that's what you're trying to do. But it won't be with me. I'm sorry, but just… please go."

"Brooke—"

"I'm so glad you found your family, and I'm happy for you, but I'm not happy to see you right now. Leave, please."

The hands he held outstretched fell to his sides. The pain in his eyes tore at her, but it didn't weaken her resolve. *So, what if he hurt, when he's done so well a job at hurting me?*

She thought she'd found her soul mate. Every moment with him up until now had been magical. They interacted as if they'd always known each other, a natural familiarity she adored.

He shoved his hands into his pockets and left. The door pulled closed behind him by an unseen force.

She sat on the bed and closed her eyes. Tears ran down her cheeks and the air seemed too thick to breathe. They'd come so close to having it all.

CHAPTER 14

KERREN

*K*erren adjusted the royal sash he'd been given to wear for Brooke's initiation. It was strange seeing the King and Queen's emblem in place of the Barrows insignia he'd grown up with.

Stranger still was, when dressed in the deep brown leather expected of his station, how much he resembled Artur.

He narrowed his eyes and applied his most serious expression. *There it is.* He was definitely Artur's son. *Perhaps if I'd spent more of my upbringing scowling, I would have seen it sooner.*

A careful knock sounded on his door, then it squeaked open. Vevina poked her head in.

"Wait," she said. "Before you kick me out."

"It's alright. Come in," he said, leaving the full-length mirror.

She entered and held out a lavish bouquet of flowers. "I returned to Earth and got these roses. I thought perhaps you could give them to Brooke."

He took the bouquet and smiled down at it. Amidst the

red roses were Leannan's tears, a cream flower which was considered the natural symbol of Weylan Barrows.

"I suppose we're stuck together again," he commented the Vevina. "And you've already set about to fix something I've mucked up."

"I'm sorry," she said. Her hair blossomed with soft pink highlights on a dark blue canvas, showing that her mood was a mixed bag. "Lorelei and I retrieved Lady Brooke this morning and it was clear that things weren't... as they should be."

"Ah." He'd gone to Brooke's room as soon as he'd woken, to try to rectify their misunderstanding, only to find her missing. "I assumed. It wouldn't be a fae ritual unless she got the full makeover, right?"

"She's gorgeous," Vevina breathed. "I wish I knew what mood I needed to be in to copy that red. Even if I had to be furious, it would probably be worth it."

He laughed and held the bouquet up, taking a deep breath of the floral scent. It smelled like Brooke, or maybe he was too busy thinking of her to notice anything else.

"Is she wearing something traditional?" He tried to imagine her in the flowing simple dresses that the Queen tended to wear to such occasions.

"Not quite. I think it's the start of a new era of fashion here," Vevina said gleefully, tugging at her own long dress. "About time, really."

He sat on the bench at the end of the bed and sighed.

"I cocked it up," he admitted.

She pursed her lips and joined him on the bench. "More than I did?"

"Quite possibly, yes."

BROOKE STOOD beside the doorway to the ballroom so that she could greet each fae in attendance as they arrived. As the Prince, Kerren was supposed to stand behind her along with Artur and Catriona, but first, he wanted his chance to greet her.

He'd entered the room from the back but made a beeline towards her, flowers at the ready. No one else had arrived yet, so if he was lucky they'd have a few moments to talk first.

"Brooke," he called.

She turned, and he nearly tripped over his own feet.

Her bright hair had been woven into the tight braids Catriona preferred, but the bottom was left to hang in loose waves. Her dress hung off her shoulders and hugged her curves before flowing out from her calves. The material was deep red but shifted to an earthy bronze depending on the light. Gold embroidery decorated the long bell sleeves as well as the neckline, which scooped low and revealed the delicious mounds of her breasts.

Clothing had rarely caught his attention before he'd met Brooke. Now he lived to see what she'd appear in next. The traditional dress of Sidera Luminis wouldn't have been suitable to her boldness. This creation embodied her well.

"You look radiant," he said once he could speak.

"Thank you," she replied cordially. Her eyes lowered to the bouquet in his hands. "Are those for me or are you accessorizing?"

He held them out to her and she took them. As she sniffed them, a genuine smile curved her lips, but only for a moment.

"They're lovely."

"Can we talk?" he asked.

"Not now..." she glanced to the doorway. "I've been told what's expected of me several hundred times. I have to focus, and the guests are arriving. We can talk later, when there's no rush."

He heard the footsteps and cursed. He hadn't arrived as early as he'd hoped, or the fae were eager to get the party started.

"Kerren," Catriona called.

He looked over his shoulder for a second then back to Brooke, who had already placed the flowers down on the gift table beside her.

"I love you," he whispered.

Her eyes closed, and she turned away from him. He couldn't tell if her reaction was good or bad, but either way, he had to step back and join the King and Queen. At least he hadn't been slapped, though. Vevina insisted that human women loved to slap men.

AT FIRST, Kerren thought he was imagining Brooke avoiding him. But now that she'd practically raced across the dance floor to escape him, he knew it wasn't in his head. She wasn't going to make an apology easy.

Artur appeared at his side and Kerren fumbled at first, resorting to the decades of programming that told him to drop everything and bow to the King. Who knew how long it would be before he thought of Artur as family. As a father.

"Your intended seems to be on a mission," Artur commented.

"She's not my intended," Kerren said somewhat bitterly.

Artur placed a hand on Kerren's shoulder. "What did you do wrong?"

"Is it that obvious?"

"Having been married for over a century, I can spot the

signs. Catriona can literally suck the noise from a room so that it's devastatingly clear when she's giving me the silent treatment," Artur confessed in a deep voice.

Kerren's lips quirked in amusement. "Yes, well… how do you fix it?"

"In your case? Wait for the embrace. You can't catch her in here, but you can catch her out there," he said, motioning outside. "Nature can hide you."

"I'm not sure a sneak attack is the wisest, and I'm not that stealthy."

"You have my blood. Shifting came naturally because you expected it. Blending into the shade and trees is easier than remaking your entire form to suit your spirit. Trust me."

Artur patted his shoulder and left. Kerren made his way outside and sat on a bench. During the embrace, Brooke would be united with the land of Sidera Luminis. She wasn't going to be claimed by a family or a person, but the spirit of the world itself.

And in everything that had happened, he hadn't even had the chance to explain it to her.

He watched everyone move in and out of the palace; Chatting, mingling, waiting for the ceremony to begin. The sun had already set, but nothing would start until the moon was above the palace.

After what seemed like forever, most of the crowd filed out into the large garden and gathered around the tree that stood central to the landscape.

Catriona and Artur guided Brooke forward and Kerren stood, the breath escaping his lungs at the sight of her again.

The tree seemed to light from within, and pixies appeared in the branches, sitting and waiting like the rest of the crowd. Catriona took Brooke's left hand and held it out towards the tree. The aurleis vines hiding in the shadows came to life and reached out to her, circling her wrist like a bracelet of lush purple blossoms.

The Queen whispered to Brooke, no doubt giving her instructions. Everyone else present understood the ceremony, but she would be in the dark.

"Do you accept the gift of the land and air, the waters and fade, and the spirit of our blood?" Artur asked.

Brooke cleared her throat, and after a quick glance to Catriona responded, "I accept this gift and offer my life's essence, that which flows through my heart. I request to be reborn into a vessel of this earth and be an instrument of her will."

"Your heart is pure, your sacrifice welcomed," Artur intoned.

Brooke stepped closer to the tree and placed her palm flat against the trunk. The vines twisted tighter and held her in place. A second passed, then she gasped.

Kerren flinched and watched as she pulled her hand away as far as the vine would allow. A thorn remained exposed on the trunk, glistening with her dark blood.

"Mortal blood to feed the past," she said with a slight whimper, holding her hand aloft and displaying the cut. "Given freely and with reverence to seal my future."

The crowd murmured thanks and bowed. Slowly, the vines released Brooke and Catriona pressed a cloth to the wound.

"We have witnessed the birth of a new daughter of Sidera Luminis. All celebrate the binding of Lady Brooke Donovan, who shall now tend the southern valleys of Weylan Barrows."

Kerren clapped along with the group. While some hated to have their land divided, he saw no issue with Brooke having a claim on a portion of the Barrows.

The majority of men and women headed inside, and Artur looked Kerren's way before heading in himself. Brooke looked up into the tree and seemed to be conversing with the pixies hiding therein.

Once the crowd had thinned he slipped into the shadows. With careful steps, he placed himself at Brooke's back.

She jumped and turned, hand to her chest. "Where did you come from?"

"Could we talk?"

"I have to head inside," she insisted.

She looked over his shoulder and into the ballroom. Music had begun to play again, giving him an idea.

"Dance with me?" he asked.

"Kerren…"

"Just one dance. I'm not trying to ruin your night," he promised. "If after one dance you're sick of me, I'll be scarce the rest of the ball."

She exhaled, brows furrowed. "Fine."

He took her by the hand that wasn't injured and led her to the dance floor. The existing occupants cleared away, giving them wide berth to dance and talk.

Placing a hand on her waist and guiding her to the rhythm, he stared into her eyes.

"I love you, Brooke," he started. She pursed her lips, but he continued, "My timing was terrible, but my intentions were honest. I had already made up my mind to tell you this before I was summoned."

"You say that," she muttered.

"It's the truth," he insisted. He spun her around and pulled her close again. "There was too much going on yesterday, and everything became muddled. I want to stay with you. Prince or not, I was ready to lay it out on the line."

"You should have said something," she hissed.

"I should have, I know. Part of me was scared that it wouldn't be approved, and part of me wondered if perhaps you were only with me because I was your only choice."

He hadn't planned on saying it, but once the words escaped his lips he heard how foolish it sounded.

"I've never been afraid before, Brooke. I didn't know how to handle it. But know that if you weren't called here, if we were back on Earth, I still would love you. And you're right—I should have told you before I told anyone else."

Her expression softened, and he bent over her to speak against her ear.

"I was bored and lonely for decades. Yet you come into my life and suddenly I see everything so clearly. You awakened me. I appreciate so much more than I did before. I see the world through your eyes, the wonder you experience, and I realize that I have missed so much."

"Kerren…"

"I don't want to miss anything else. I want to share every minute with you. I can't imagine my life with anyone else, and I don't want to. There is no one more perfect for me than you," he confessed.

Something wet brushed his cheek, making him pull back. Light reflected off the trails of tears falling over Brooke's face.

"I've made you cry," he whispered.

"Damnit," she said with a soft laugh. "Yes, you have. Because I needed to know this. I needed to know that you'd be happy here, or there, or wherever. I needed to know that I was enough for you."

"Of course, you are."

"Then my answer is yes," she said.

He blinked in confusion then stopped dancing. "Yes?"

"Yes. It's been so fast, and so crazy, but yes. I've never been more certain of anything than this—I want to marry you," she said, fresh tears falling.

He wiped the moisture from her cheeks with his thumbs

and bent over her, pulling her into a kiss. Drawing back, he laughed.

"Oh… Euphrasie said to call her if you needed anything."

Brooke arched a brow. "That… she… of course. I can't believe you went to Euphrasie."

"I didn't. Vevina did for me."

"That makes so much more sense," Brooke murmured.

"Pardon me," Catriona interrupted. "Since you too have finally come to your senses, Brooke, I wanted to discuss your future employment."

"Right now?" Kerren asked. "We've just—"

"Brooke expressed a sincere desire to be involved in her future, which means yes, right now, because it's the right moment," Catriona said firmly.

Brooke eyed him before stepping away. "I'll be back."

"I'll be waiting."

EPILOGUE

BROOKE

Fae weddings were nothing like the weddings celebrated by the humans of Earth. The vow exchange didn't make anyone sleepy, there was no white dress. No rings to exchange and no bridesmaids or groomsmen.

Just promises of love, ceremonial blood-letting, and lots of drinking.

Brooke had absolutely no complaints.

Well, on second thought, she could always do without blood-letting.

She wandered through the garden of partying guests, one hand on her extended belly. The fae saw no fault in her marrying while already swollen and pregnant, and the lack of judgment was a huge relief.

On the contrary, this would be the first fae birth in the last five years, so she was overladen with congratulations and well-wishing.

She wasn't due for another few months, but she'd taken time off from her job until then.

"There you are," Vevina said with a hint of playful frustration. She held out a plate of fruit and sweets, scolding, "Eat before you pass out."

Brooke took the assortment of finger foods with a sigh of relief. "Thank you. I've been too busy greeting everyone from here to the isles."

"And farther. You've got guests from off-world, dear. But save the socializing skills for your job," Vevina teased. "Damn. I need to run. I can't find Kerren... I think he's using his magic to hide in the bushes."

Brooke watched Vevina rush off. As she munched a honeyed cracker, she waved to a group of dragon shifters from another planet.

The Queen had made Brooke an official ambassador for the fae, and though she primarily secured relations between Sidera Luminis and Earth, she also interacted with the many other planets. Kerren often joined her, and if not, she went with Vevina, who she'd found the heart to fully forgive.

"It's been centuries since we had twins," a woman mused.

Brooke turned to see a petite and curvy fae staring at her stomach. "Excuse me?"

"May I?" the woman asked, extending her hand.

Brooke always thought she'd hate strangers touching her stomach, but the fae seemed to leave pleasant tickles of magic, and they adored children, so the aversion had quickly vanished.

"Sure," she replied.

The woman gently pressed her fingertips to Brooke's large stomach. A smile grew on the stranger's lips and a soft glow emitted from her entire form.

"Yes. Twins. Strong and eager to meet the world," she whispered.

Brooke rubbed her belly. "Are you sure?"

The woman nodded.

"Brooke," Kerren called.

Brooke turned and saw Kerren making his way over. Glancing back, she didn't see the stranger anywhere. Kerren came close and gave her a quick peck on the cheek.

"If we've both made rounds, perhaps we could find someplace quiet?" he asked lifting his brows suggestively.

"Wait… someone just said we're having twins." Brooke's eyes searched the crowds around them to no avail. "But she disappeared."

"Twins?" He placed his hands on her and dropped to his knees. With his cheek against her stomach, he glanced up. "Do you know how rare that is? How blessed we are?"

"Well, yes, I can imagine," she said slowly. "But who was that woman?"

Kerren closed his eyes and seemed to be listening to the babies.

"Kerren!"

His eyes popped open. "Ah. What did she look like?"

"Short…curvy like me. Long pink hair and eyes."

"Fianni." He stood and wrapped an arm around her. "It's not her original name, but current. She's the aspect of Harmony. If she touched you, she blessed our children."

"Wow."

"Will you ever get tired of being surprised?" he asked.

"Never."

He kissed her forehead and ran his fingers through her long hair. "Brooke Donovan, I will never tire of any part of you. Especially the way you make love to food."

She slapped his arm and giggled. "Speaking of making love…"

The scene around them faded as he pulled them both into the shadows. They were hidden from everyone, and he led her far from the party to a clearing beyond the trees. He released the cloak around them, bringing the world back into brightness.

"I must be the luckiest man in the world," he said, nuzzling her neck.

"Probably," she agreed.

He sighed. "You make it hard to give an honest compliment."

"What can I say? I like it hard."

ABOUT THE AUTHOR

Godiva Glenn is a nocturnal being, much like vampires and cats. She specializes in weaving paranormal romance fiction that transports readers into enchanting worlds where love and the supernatural collide. Her catalog spans shifters, fae, demons, and more.

She grew up surrounded by books thanks to her grandfather, an avid reader himself. Through weekly trips to the library, she devoured books, from adventures in babysitting to worlds of magical knights and powerful queens. However, it wasn't until she read her first romance novel in her early twenties that her creative spirit caught fire. She realized that she absolutely needed to give life to her own characters and worlds, and she embarked on a journey to become an author.

Godiva lives in the U.S. with dreams of traveling abroad to research locations in person.

Also, she does not bite and is relatively pleasant to socialize with.

For updates, sneak peeks, and exclusive content, join Godiva's mailer: www.godivaglenn.com/sign-up/

ALSO BY GODIVA GLENN

~NIGHT WOLVES~

Night Revelations

Night Born

Night Surrender

Night Caught

Night Forgiven

Night Stolen

Visit GodivaGlenn.com for the full catalogue!